She'd hurt him by pulling away.

She wanted to apologize...but maybe it would be better this way, if they both behaved as if this was just like any other job. Protect the client, find the bad guy and go home. After the way she had bailed on him, only a fool would believe that things could ever go back to the way they had been between them.

Then she was a fool, because even in the face of overwhelming odds, she wanted to believe it. And that more than anything said she couldn't spend the next few days with him.

"Someone will be with you 24/7."

"Someone or you?" Her tone came out terse.

"Don't worry, Jen. I get it. You don't want to be with me. But I will head up your detail."

What choice did she have?

If she wanted to help the children and live to tell about it, then she'd have to let Ethan back into her life no matter how difficult it would be for them both.

Books by Susan Sleeman

Love Inspired Suspense

High-Stakes Inheritance
Behind the Badge
The Christmas Witness
*Double Exposure

*The Justice Agency

SUSAN SLEEMAN

grew up in a small Wisconsin town where she spent her summers reading Nancy Drew and developing a love of mystery and suspense books. Today she channels this enthusiasm into hosting the popular internet website *TheSuspenseZone.com* and writing romantic-suspense and mystery novels.

Much to her husband's chagrin, Susan loves to look at everyday situations and turn them into murder-and-mayhem scenarios for future novels. If you've met Susan, she has probably figured out a plausible way to kill you and get away with it.

Susan currently lives in Florida, but has had the pleasure of living in nine states. Her husband is a church music director and they have two beautiful daughters, a very special son-in-law and an adorable grandson. To learn more about Susan, please visit www.SusanSleeman.com.

DOUBLE EXPOSURE

Susan Sleeman

Love Inspired

™ LOVE INSPIRED BOOKS

ISBN-13: 978-0-373-67516-6

DOUBLE EXPOSURE

Copyright © 2012 by Susan Sleeman

www.LoveInspiredBooks.com

Printed in U.S.A.

For all have sinned, and fall short of the glory of God, and all are justified freely by his grace through the redemption that came by Jesus Christ.
—*Romans* 3:23, 24

For Don, Mickey and Barb Sleeman and Patti Ramirez, who support my writing and promote my books with great enthusiasm. Thanks cannot begin to describe my appreciation, but thank you.

Acknowledgments

Additional thanks to:

My family; My ever-patient and understanding husband, Mark. My daughter Emma for all the help with plot issues and Erin for your graphic-design expertise.

My patient, sweet and talented editor, Tina James. I am thrilled at the opportunity to work with and learn from you. And thank you for continuing to have faith in my writing.

My friend Judy Peterson for her insight into adoption. Thank you for your patience and diligence in answering my questions. For being open and sharing your personal experiences with me so that I could understand the emotions involved in adoption.

The very generous Ron Norris—retired police officer with the LaVerne Police Department—who gives of his time and knowledge in both police procedures as well as weapons information. Thank you for always answering my questions so thoroughly and so promptly. You go above and beyond, and I can't thank you enough! Any errors in or liberties taken with the technical details Ron so patiently explained to me are all my doing.

And most important, thank You, God, for my faith and for giving me daily challenges to grow closer to You.

ONE

Someone threatened to kill her last night. Now a man was following her.

Coincidence? Not likely.

Jennie Buchanan's breath hitched as she boarded Portland's MAX light-rail train and wound through standing passengers toward the far door. She glanced back.

The guy crept in. Searching the car, he caught sight of her and headed down the narrow aisle.

Her photographer's eye took in every detail. Short, stocky, wearing a light gray hoodie, twenty-five at the oldest, he looked like one of the many skaters hanging out at Pioneer Square. His eyes told a different story. Dark and narrowed, fixed on her like a hunter sighting prey.

He advanced. Silent. Stalking. One hand never leaving his hoodie pocket.

Had to be a weapon. A gun, maybe, or a knife.

Fear razored through her stomach, and she backed deeper into the car. She tripped on a baby stroller, grabbed the handle and righted herself. The fresh scent rising up from the sweet baby did nothing to calm her fears.

"Sorry," she said to the mother, her voice trembling. She tried to smile an apology, too, but her mouth wouldn't cooperate.

She couldn't endanger the baby so she kept moving, easing in and out of people. She ached to ask them for help. The tall man with a kind face. A young woman, earbuds snugged in her ears and tapping her foot, her face buried in a book like many of the other commuters.

Not a good idea. What could she say? How could she make them believe she was in danger when even she didn't know why?

She searched for an escape route before the train departed, but the doors grated on their hinges and closed with a solid thud. She had no way out. Her heart picked up speed, thudding in her ears, a rapid *thump, thump, thump* as her brain clouded with indecision.

Please, God. Send a police officer. Even a transit cop would be good. Anyone official, really. Just someone in uniform to scare him off.

He continued to move closer. Slower now. Stealthily, like a hunting cat. He flipped up his hood, his face dark and shadowed. Who was he? And what did he have planned?

He came to a stop on the other side of the car. He looked up and the overhead light gave her a clear look at his dark eyes boring into her.

The train jerked on its rails. A high-pitched squeal

grated up her nerves. Riders jostled. She lost her footing for a moment. So did he, wobbling then reaching up to clamp stubby fingers around a slick aluminum pole.

She gasped.

His fingers. His hand. Stained bright red, the color running down the underside of his sleeve. Paint. Red paint.

The same color used in the art gallery break-in last night where someone had ripped her photos from the wall and spray-painted a message.

OPEN THE SHOW AND YOU DIE! it said.

She hadn't seen the warning, but the gallery owner had phoned first thing this morning. She'd said the police wanted to talk to her, but Jennie was photographing a six-alarm fire for the newspaper so they agreed to interview her later. Jennie had spent the past two hours waffling between breathing in caustic smoke and wondering if these creeps would kill her if she went through with the show designed to raise money for her charity Photos of Hope.

Would it actually come to that?

She glanced at the guy again. Cold, deadly eyes peered out from the shadow of his hood.

Yeah, when she didn't cancel the fundraiser, he'd make good on the threat. And she wouldn't cancel. Of that, he could be sure. Her charity supported impoverished children and many would suffer without the money she raised for medicine and food. The children came first. They always came first.

But he couldn't possibly know they'd already decided to hold the show as scheduled. Only she, the gallery owner and the police knew, right? So why was he coming after her now?

He shifted, eyes raking her body. Drilling into her face as if he were mining her thoughts. Maybe he did know, and he was here to end her life.

Easy, Jennie. It's broad daylight. People around. He's not going to hurt you here.

Right?

Maybe.

She had no idea what he intended.

She wanted to bolt through the car to move far away from those piercing eyes.

Stay calm. Two more stops. Just two more stops.

Then what? Get off the train and become an easier target?

She needed help. She should call 9-1-1. And what? Tell them a man with red paint on his hands was following her? By the time she convinced them to respond, she'd be dead.

Think, Jennie. Think.

Her phone pealed from her pocket, the shrill ring making her jump. She turned away from her stalker's cold stare and looked at the screen. Madeline. The gallery owner.

"Thank goodness you called," Jennie whispered into her phone. "Someone's following me. He has red paint on his hand and jacket. I think he's the guy who broke into the gallery last night." Her words tumbled over each other.

"Where are you?" Madeline sounded calm, as usual.

"On MAX. First car. Two stops away." Anxiety made it hard to breathe. She paused and sucked in stale air but still felt light-headed.

"Ethan Justice is here. I'll send him to meet your train."

"Ethan." Of course! Ethan! Madeline had hired his P.I. agency to investigate the break-in and keep them safe.

Thank You, God.

"Stay on the phone," Madeline continued. "I'll give it to him and he can talk to you on his way there."

As the train slowed for the next stop and passengers stirred, Jennie heard Madeline relay details to Ethan. The doors opened, and she stepped aside to let people pass. Her hooded tail stayed put. His eyes never leaving her, the razor-sharp gaze terrifying.

"I'm on my way, Jen." Ethan's voice, warm and familiar, rumbling through the phone, sent relief flooding down her veins, the last reaction she expected for the man she'd walked out on ten years ago.

"He's after me, Ethan," she whispered.

"I can't hear you, Jen. Too much background noise."

"I don't want anyone to hear me," she said a bit louder. "It'll quiet down in here when we start moving again."

"I'll wait."

That was Ethan. Patient and caring. Coming to

the rescue of a woman who'd hurt him. Hurt him badly. And yet here he was. On his way to stop the creep whose scowl said he'd kill her without a second thought.

She shivered, a long shudder working over the length of her body. She wrapped her free arm around her stomach and waited for the train to reach cruising speed. When the car settled into a soft, rhythmic hum, she cupped her hand over her mouth and phone.

"There's a man," she said. "He followed me from the fire."

"Are you sure he followed you?" Ethan breathed fast, as if running.

"Yes. I was shooting pictures as I walked to keep my mind off the break-in. I caught him in the viewfinder a few times. I was already freaked out from hearing about last night so I wondered if he was tailing me."

She quickly looked to see if he still stood there. Fierce and threatening, he hadn't moved.

"I got on the closest MAX car," she went on. "Ran through it and back outside. Then I boarded the next car. He did the same thing."

Ethan mumbled something she couldn't make out. A loud exhale followed. "Madeline said something about paint."

"Red. On his hand and jacket. I didn't see it until he got close."

"What's he doing now?"

She glanced at him again. "Just watching me. But

I'm afraid, Ethan." Saying it aloud sent another shiver down her body. "I think he might have a gun. He hasn't taken his hand out of his jacket pocket this whole time."

"Calm down, Jen. Panicking might make him do something crazy." He paused and she heard him draw in air. "I'm almost there. You should be able to see me soon. I'm wearing a long-sleeved white shirt and jeans."

As if she needed to know his attire. Even with this creep threatening her life, she'd instantly recognize someone she'd once loved.

"Madeline said you were in the first car," he continued. "Wave when you see me."

"Okay." She peered out the window, searching for the man she hadn't seen since their amazing summer vacation from college. Hadn't seen since the night she'd lied and told him that she just didn't love him and didn't want to be in a relationship with him anymore.

She'd never forgotten his face that night. Shocked, surprised, but most of all hurt. So hurt. She still felt horrible about lying to him. She had a choice and had taken the easy way out. Rejecting him had seemed less painful than waiting for his rejection when he learned about her past. That would end their relationship anyway, so why wait? So much easier to end things before she fell even more in love with him.

Now he was committed to helping her.

In the distance, she saw him running, dodging people on the busy downtown sidewalk. She took in his lean, wide-shouldered build, square jaw and dark hair cut shorter than she remembered. The white shirt set off his dark coloring, making him look dangerous yet very appealing at the same time.

The train began to slow and she waved to let him know she saw him.

He stood tall and strong where her train would disembark. "Where's the guy standing in relationship to you?"

She checked to make sure he hadn't moved. "Behind me. A little to my left. Near the other door."

"Describe him."

"Hispanic. Short. Stocky. Wearing a light gray hoodie. He has the hood up."

The train's automated voice announced their pending stop and they slowed to a crawl.

"I see him," Ethan said. "When the doors open, I'll come forward and I want you to run out and get behind me. Okay?"

"Yes."

"I'm gonna hang up now to keep my hands free."

She nodded her understanding and slid her phone into her pocket. His hands came to rest at his sides, as he settled into a centered stance, clearly poised and ready for anything. Probably an unconscious habit from years at the FBI.

She was so thankful for his law-enforcement training. Despite the years they'd been apart, it was immediately obvious how strong and capable he was. He'd probably been a wonderful agent—just as she'd always known he'd be. She wasn't surprised when she read in the paper that Ethan and his four siblings followed through on their high-school pact. They'd decided to serve in law enforcement to show their appreciation and respect for their adoptive dad, who was a retired cop.

She *was* surprised, shocked really, when she read the rest of the article about an intruder murdering their adoptive parents. The local police department couldn't solve the case so the five of them left their jobs to hunt down the killer and then stayed together to form the Justice Agency.

If someone wanted to hurt her, she could think of no better allies than Ethan and his siblings.

Brakes squealed as the train slowed even more. This was it. Time to escape this creep.

Her palms grew moist. She scrubbed them over her jeans, stained and sooty from the six-alarm fire. She glanced back to check on her tail. He was on the move. Slowly inching toward her.

"C'mon, open, open, open," she whispered to the doors, but kept her eyes on him.

His hand came out of his pocket. Something slid through his palm and between his fingers. Looked like a knife. A switchblade. Closed. But easily opened with a flick of his fingers. He took a few more steps.

The train jerked to a stop. She lost her balance, wobbled and worked to regain her footing. She braced for the attack she feared was imminent.

His footfalls thumped slowly across the metal floor.

Close now. Too close.

Please, God, please! Let me get to Ethan before this guy hurts me.

The doors whooshed apart, but not before she heard a click. Not any click, but the distinctive snap of his switchblade opening a whisper of a space behind her back.

Ethan bolted forward. He saw the thug move toward Jennie as she stepped off the train and merged into the crowd. A steady stream of passengers kept Ethan separated from her. The hooded guy kept pace with her.

"Jen, he's right behind you," Ethan yelled as he shoved through the people rushing at him.

She looked back.

Everything seemed to unfold in front of Ethan in slow motion.

The riders' chatter, their footfalls on concrete were merely a fog of noise as he bumped through them like a pinball in a machine. But he didn't have the speed of a pinball. He couldn't move fast enough.

Please, God. I need to get to her.

The guy's hands shot out. One held a knife, the blade glinting in the sun.

"No-o-o," Ethan screamed and felt a chill despite the blazing summer sun.

The guy grabbed her camera bag, worn cross-body. A flick of his knife and he sliced clean through the strap. He gave a powerful tug. Jennie wrapped the strap around her hand and hugged the bag to her chest. They struggled.

"Stop," Ethan yelled.

The guy glanced up. Hard, black eyes warred with a decision. He let go of the bag and bolted away.

Jennie lurched back and plummeted toward a concrete planter, her head inches from serious injury.

Ethan sent his body airborne, diving toward the sidewalk. He hit the ground on his side, his breath exploding on impact. He reached out to cradle her body and protect her head, his shoulder sandpapering along rough pavement.

"Ethan," she said, her voice soft and vulnerable.

The planter bit into his back and the sidewalk tore the flesh on his upper arm. He felt the wet flow of blood across his skin as pain screamed into his body. He ignored the sting, clamping his hands on his forearms and holding fast to Jennie.

Her body rotated as he slid. She groaned.

A few more feet of his skin burning on concrete and they came to a stop, her back pressed to his chest, his arms circling her waist.

"You okay?" he whispered, his breath stirring her hair. The sweet scent of fresh coconuts unleashed a flood of memories from the summer they'd shared at the beach.

"Yes."

Thank You, Father.

A crowd surrounded them, chattering, speculating, her attacker missing in the sea of faces peering down.

Ethan released her, coming to his feet in one fluid move to search the crowd for her assailant.

He spotted him boarding the train just before the doors closed with a solid thud. Keeping him in view until the train eased away, Ethan committed details to memory for the police report. He turned back to Jennie. She'd come to a sitting position, eyes wide. Still frightened. Maybe heading toward shock.

He wanted to scoop her into his arms. Hold her close, push away her fear and promise to protect her. He fisted his hands instead. Given the way she'd left him that summer between his junior and senior year of college, touching her would likely have the opposite effect of the soothing one he intended. Plus, if he was going to protect her until they located her assailant, he needed to keep things on a professional level.

He squatted down next to her and kept his tone soft. "Are you sure you're okay?"

"Is he gone?" Her gaze tracked up and down the sidewalk.

"He's on the train."

She shuddered, and her face relaxed a bit.

"Can you stand?" he asked, hoping to move her out of the curious crowd and inside, away from danger.

"I think so," she said, but he could hear doubt in her voice.

He stood, his body screaming in protest as the adrenaline started to wear off and pain set in. Stifling a groan, he held out his hand, smiling to help ease the terror lodged on her face.

Icy fingers slipped into his, her other hand still clutching the camera case. Their eyes met. Ten years melted away to that balmy summer night at his family's beach house in Seaside and his parents' anniversary party.

She'd stood there so appealing in a daring red dress. Innocently unaware of her beauty. Huge brown eyes captivating him and attracting other men within her radius.

Man, what a night. Excitement in the air. His surprise threatening to burst out. Fighting to control it. Waiting for the right moment to tell her that he planned to transfer colleges to be closer to where she went to school. Her throwing cold water on him, telling him not to bother—she wasn't into him.

And now, here she was, rising up to meet him, and no matter what he felt, he had to focus on keeping her safe.

Still holding his hand, she took a few steps, as if checking for injuries.

"Everything okay?" he asked.

She let go and, eyes clouded, lifted her bag. "I am, but I don't know about my camera."

Good. If she was concerned for her camera, maybe she wasn't as close to a breakdown as he'd thought.

"C'mon. Let's get out of here." With a hand on her back, he urged her along the sidewalk, heading toward the gallery.

"Shouldn't we call the police?" she asked.

"Let's get inside first. Then we'll report it." He took

the side near the road and kept his head on a swivel, looking for any threat. He didn't really think he'd try something again so soon, but Ethan couldn't take any chances.

They moved at a good clip despite Jennie's limp. She had to be in pain, but she didn't complain. Didn't speak at all. She cradled her camera bag like a baby, and her focus remained fixed ahead.

During their summer together, he'd been able to read her mind, but today? Not a clue. Was she thinking about the assault or their breakup?

Did she feel the awkwardness of their reunion, now that the moment of danger had passed? There was no way for him to know. Still, he could make sure she knew he'd let go of his anger over the way she'd bailed on him and was up to the task of protecting her.

"It's good to see you again, Jen," he said, keeping his tone light and sincere.

She looked up at him, a tight little smile the only outward indication of her mood.

"Thanks for helping me today. I don't know what I would've done if…" She shook her head, then reached up and fingered his tattered sleeve. "I haven't even asked if you're okay."

He looked at her slender fingers brushing over the white fabric soaked with his blood. Her concern warmed him and he wanted to bask in it for a few moments, but he couldn't afford to be distracted.

"I'm fine, Jen." He lifted her hand from his arm and gave a quick squeeze before releasing it.

"But your shoulder looks bad. There's a lot of blood." She stared up at him, measuring. Weighing.

"It's just a scratch. I'll look at it when we get to the gallery."

Her concern washed away and her face paled.

Nice one, Ethan. Remind her of the threat waiting for her.

"Everything will be all right. I promise."

"I really hope so."

"We'll do everything within our power to find this guy."

"Good. Because no matter what he threatens, I won't cancel the benefit. This is our biggest fund-raiser of the year. I won't let these children down." Her shoulders went back, and she tilted her chin in the cute little stubborn angle he remembered so well. She was still so determined. Tough, ready to take on the world. Now she directed it toward helping children.

Since she'd moved to Portland five years ago, he'd read all about her dedication to Photos of Hope, the charity she had founded and on which she now served as chairman of the board. She traveled the world, shooting pictures of suffering children then displaying them in posh galleries to raise money for them. And thanks to Madeline, it was now his job to make sure she lived to carry out her work.

They turned the corner and the gallery came into view. A crime-scene van pulled from the curb and yellow tape strung across the sidewalk fluttered in the breeze.

The sun darted behind heavy clouds and a dark shadow descended over them. He saw Jennie shudder. The urge to comfort her rose up stronger than before, but nothing he could do would spare her from the destruction and the chilling message declaring if she didn't cancel the show she'd be killed.

TWO

As they neared the Premier Gallery, Jennie looked down at her feet.

Right. Left. Repeat. Focus. Keep moving. Stop thinking. Don't dwell on the trashed gallery or the message or Ethan. Definitely not Ethan.

She felt him next to her as if they were connected. His strength and confidence giving her hope that this would end soon. And if it didn't, that he'd be there for her. He'd already put his life on the line for her, circling his arms around her, bearing the brunt of injury, but now that all the unresolved issues of their past and the painful way they'd once parted came rushing back, she wished he'd go away.

What kind of person was she to want him gone when he was willing to sacrifice his life for her?

A scared person, that's what. Scared of this threat against her life. Scared of the way her heart beat quicker in his presence. Scared of caving in to her fear of this lunatic and failing the children.

A clue, Lord, just give me a clue what to do here. How to act. How to survive. You've brought me

*through some crazy times in the past. I need You to
do the same thing now.*

"Are you sure you're up to seeing this?" Ethan
clasped the gallery's door handle.

"I have to see it sometime, right?"

"Madeline's already told you what happened. We
could come back after she's had a chance to clean up."

"No," she said, surprised at the strength in her voice.
"I can't run away from this."

He watched her for a few moments, his eyes searching until he seemed to shake off his thoughts and
opened the door.

She stepped inside and came to a stop. A caustic
paint odor saturated the narrow room where she'd once
found comfort. Now order had turned to chaos. Shards
of glass, mangled frames and torn photos littered the
rough brick floor. Black-and-white. Color. It made no
difference. This creep had ripped her photos of children from the wall without a care.

She could feel the vandal's presence. Strong and
threatening, like on the train. She saw him, standing here in the dim light of night, shredding the pictures and tossing them around like bits of confetti.
Then moving to the wall. His arms sweeping in big,
powerful strokes, anger seething from his face and
vibrating through his hands as the spray can spit out
his message.

OPEN THE SHOW AND YOU DIE!

She stared at it. Expected fear to rise up again, but
anger boiled up instead. How dare he do this to Pho-

tos of Hope! The funds from the sale of those pictures were supposed to help children. Starving children. Sick children.

"Jennifer, there you are," gallery owner Madeline St. James called out as she hurried toward them. She wore a deep fuchsia pantsuit that didn't hide the fashionably thin woman's hard angles. "Are you all right?"

"I'm fine."

"Don't worry about the mess." Madeline waved a hand in the air as if the destruction was of no consequence to her. "The police have just given me the go-ahead to clean up. I'm phoning staff members to come in this afternoon. We'll have this place righted in no time and open the show on schedule."

"I appreciate your hard work, Madeline," Jennie said, but Madeline was already turning toward Ethan.

"And you, Ethan?" She pointed at his arm. "That looks like a nasty injury."

"It's nothing. We're both fine." His reassuring tone gave Jennie hope that he had everything under control.

"I trust you're still on board with the protection details we discussed earlier." Madeline raised a thin eyebrow.

"Yes," Ethan answered, but he didn't look enthusiastic about it.

"You don't sound very convincing."

"Like I told you before, I don't have to personally see to Jennie's detail. Everyone at the firm is capable of handling it."

Madeline patted his good arm, diamond rings glinting in the spotlight. "I dearly love all of your brothers and sisters, Ethan, but none of them have the extensive background you have, now do they?"

"They may not have as many years in the law-enforcement game, but they're pros."

"You know me, Ethan. I hire only the best, and as I've told you repeatedly, you're the best." Her lips tipped in a slight smile. "You're not planning on disappointing me, are you?"

"No," he said, reluctance still in his tone.

Jennie wasn't surprised at Madeline's stance. Jennie had encountered similar stubbornness while planning this show with Madeline. When the woman made up her mind about something, there was no point in arguing. She always got her way.

"Fine, then if you'll excuse me, I'll get back to work." She made a sharp pivot on spiked heels and headed for the back of the gallery.

Jennie saw Ethan fist his hands. He clearly didn't want to be with her. The sooner they got to the bottom of all of this, the sooner he would be on his way.

Sucking in a reedy breath, she squatted down to pick through tattered photos, searching for anything left intact.

"I don't know how anyone could do this," she said to Ethan as he hovered over her like a solicitous parent. "Without the money from the fundraiser, many of the children we help could die."

"Then we need to make sure that doesn't happen."

He sounded so confident and sure. "And we'll start by figuring out who did this."

"This?" She gestured at the devastation surrounding her. "*This* makes no sense. How do we even begin to figure it out?"

"We take things one step at a time." His voice remained calm and even.

How could he be so levelheaded when chaos surrounded them? When they were back together after all these years?

"You mentioned seeing your attacker through your camera," he went on. "Did you take any pictures of him?"

"Several."

"Good. We can run them through facial-recognition software to see if he's in the database. If he is, we'll have his ID in less than an hour."

"I hate that people like this guy are willing to destroy things intended to do so much good." She stood, putting distance between her and the picture scraps.

"This isn't about destruction, Jen. It's about stopping the show." He paused and watched her as if waiting for his comment to settle in.

"What I don't get is why. I mean, why trash this place and why try to take my camera?"

"I doubt this guy followed you all that way simply to steal your camera."

"So why'd he try it, then?"

"I think he's after a memory card and he thought it would be in the bag."

She looked at him, eyebrow raised, and waited for an explanation.

"Look," he said. "A crime like this one is often financially motivated, but no one stands to make money if the show doesn't open. So we have to look at other motives."

"Such as?"

"My first thought was someone was out for revenge, and I'm still not ruling that out. Our team is already investigating gallery and charity staff, looking for anyone who might have a grudge against Photos of Hope or the gallery itself."

He paused and moved closer. "But now that this guy tried to steal your camera bag, we have to consider what the break-in and attempted theft have in common. Maybe we need to expand our investigation to include the pictures themselves."

"What could my pictures have to do with this?"

"If you accidentally caught someone doing something they don't want displayed in public, that person would try to stop you from showing the pictures. And that would mean destroying not only the pictures, but preventing you from producing more copies."

"That could be true of someone with a personal grudge, too."

"Agreed, and that's why we'll continue to look at all avenues. But if we start by reviewing the pictures, we can quickly see if my theory holds any weight, and if not, we can rule it out."

"There's just one problem. I only use a digital for-

mat for the newspaper. I use film for all other work."
She gestured at the jumble of frames and torn photos
at her feet. "You're looking at the only copies of these
pictures. All I have are the negatives."

"So how long will it take to reprint them?"

"I'll be lucky to finish before the show."

"And there's no way to speed that up?"

"No, but I could have the negatives drum scanned
to create digital copies. Scanning would only take a
few hours and you could view the pictures on a computer while I work on reprints for the show."

"Good. Good." A burst of enthusiasm lit his eyes.
"But first we'll email the photo of your attacker to
Cole. He'll have someone at the marshal's office run
it." She remembered reading his brother Cole had once
worked as a U.S. Marshal in fugitive investigations.

"We can upload the pictures on my computer. It's
in the break area." Ethan put his hand on her back and
gently urged her to move.

Heat radiated through his fingers and a small gasp
of surprise slipped out of her. Reacting to him every
time he touched her was not good. So until she learned
to control her response, she couldn't be with him any
more than necessary. She moved away, and his hand
fell to his side.

"The negatives are at my house," she said, searching for any reason to put distance between them. "I
could save time by picking them up while you email
the digital pictures." She held out her camera but he
snagged her elbow instead.

"*We'll* get your negatives, Jen. Together. After we email Cole. You won't go anywhere alone until we neutralize this threat." He sounded so professional. So detached.

Clearly, she'd hurt him by pulling away. She wanted to apologize…but maybe it would be better this way, if they both behaved as if this was just a job to him. A job like any other job. Protect the client, find the bad guy and go home.

After the way she'd bailed on him, only a fool would believe that things could ever go back to the way they had been between them.

Then she was a fool because even in the face of overwhelming odds, she wanted to believe it.

Seeing him again, his smile, his strength, the un-wavering confidence, made her want him to care. And that, more than anything, said she couldn't spend time with him. It wouldn't end well, for either of them.

She opened her mouth to object to his plan, but he said, "Until this is resolved, someone will be with you 24/7."

"Someone, or you?" Her tone came out terse.

"Don't worry, Jen. I get it. You don't want to be with me." She thought she heard a hint of sadness in his voice, but his face remained impassive. "You heard Madeline. She insists I head up your detail and she's an old family friend so I won't disappoint her."

Of course he wouldn't. She'd once fallen for this Ethan. An honorable man even when it caused him pain. Not that she could presume to know how he felt about being around her. It had been years since she could read his every expression. But still, it couldn't be easy for him to work with her, could it?

She'd try to give him an out. "I respect your desire to help Madeline. Really I do. But I'm sure you could convince her to let someone else from the agency work with me instead."

"No." His dark eyes dared her to challenge him and his adamant tone left her speechless.

The Ethan she'd known had been more laid-back, but that was before his stint with the FBI and before his parents were murdered.

She hated to see the way pain and harsh experiences had hardened him, but she couldn't deny that his new fierce determination was attractive—too attractive.

Her work was her priority—she couldn't let any chance of a relationship get in the way of that. Especially not a relationship with Ethan, which would be doomed to failure if he ever learned about her past. It would be far wiser to avoid him.

But what choice did she have?

None.

If she wanted to help the children and live to tell about it, then she'd have to let Ethan back into her life no matter how difficult it would be for them both.

In the gallery's refreshment area, Ethan slid onto a chair across the table from Jennie. She opened her camera and pulled out her memory card. He glanced back at his computer, watching it run through the start-up screens, and tried to concentrate on the job at hand.

Focus on the threat. Keep things professional.

Yeah, right. Easier said than done.

Especially when she held out the memory card and searched his face. He'd have to be blind not to see the hope these pictures brought. She believed they would lead straight to her attacker and end the case so she wouldn't have to spend time with him.

He wasn't as optimistic.

A good lead? Maybe. *If* it panned out. But finding the man's picture in the database was a long shot.

He took the card, and when his computer chimed, signaling the end of boot up, he entered his password. He inserted the card into the slot. "You want me to sort through the pictures or do you want to do it?"

"I have a ton of pics on there, so it'll be faster if I do it."

He slid the computer across the table, and she went straight to work.

Her knee bounced as if she couldn't wait to get out of here. He took the time to study her face. The sweet, soft face he'd once thought would grow old alongside his.

Not that it mattered. Not one bit. They'd never get together again.

Even if she wanted to, which she clearly didn't, she'd left him once. She'd do the same thing again. After his ex-fiancée, Carla, had bailed on him, he'd sworn off dating. Let other men be taken in by promises women made. He was done with that. So done.

She ejected her card then pushed the computer back to him. "I saved all the pictures of him in a folder on your desktop."

As she put the card back in her camera, he opened the first picture and sought out details he'd not caught when watching the guy.

Hard eyes. Experienced eyes. A criminal's eyes. His attack on Jennie wasn't his first such act. Wouldn't be his last. Ethan clicked through the others. In an early one before he'd put up his hood, she'd caught something unusual on the back of his neck.

Ethan enlarged the picture. A tattoo with a scrolling *S* in bright red ended with a vivid green snake's head, mouth open and tongue extended at the base of the guy's neck.

"Did you see this tattoo?" Ethan asked.

She shook her head, and he swiveled the computer so she could see.

Her knee calmed, and she stared at the screen. "I've seen a tattoo like that before."

"You remember where?"

"Yeah. A worker at Photos of Hope's distribution center had one in the exact same place."

"I didn't know your charity was large enough to have distribution centers."

"Just one. In Brownsville, Texas. When Photos of Hope started, we gave all the money we raised to other charities, and that still works well in the United

States. But with all the corruption in Mexico, if we want to be sure the right people receive help, we have to purchase and distribute the items ourselves. So a few years ago, we obtained the necessary permits to distribute food, household items and medical supplies. We still have problems with corruption and supplies not getting where they're intended, but it's on a much smaller scale."

"So this guy works in Brownsville, then."

"Yes."

"And you're sure his tattoo matches the one in this picture?" Ethan pointed at the screen.

"Positive. I even talked to the warehouse manager about it. This isn't the kind of image I want to portray for the charity."

Ethan was starting to get excited. "Firing him could be motive enough for revenge."

"We didn't fire him. The manager said he was one of her best workers. Since he's not in the public eye, she didn't think he'd have an impact on our image. I trust her judgment, so as far as I know, he still works there."

"While I finish up here, I'd like you to find out everything you can about him from the manager."

"You think this worker has something to do with the break-in?"

"It isn't a common tattoo, and I doubt it's a coincidence that he has the same one as your attacker." He didn't add that he also felt confident the tattoo marked him as a gang member. No need to share that thought until they proved this was gang related.

Jennie took out her phone, and he set to work on his emails. He heard her chatting with the manager but he focused on his task. He not only emailed Cole, but copied the message to his sister Kat, as well. As a former Portland police officer, she had contacts in the department who could tell them if this particular tattoo linked Jennie's assailant to a gang. He attached the pictures and hit Send, watching as the message disappeared from his screen.

"His name is Javier Caldera," Jennie said, clapping her phone closed. "He still works at the warehouse. My manager says he's an exemplary employee, and she highly doubts he could have anything to do with this."

"We still need to investigate him, Jen. People do things you'd never expect." He flinched as he realized, too late, his statement's double meaning.

If she caught his reference to the way she'd bailed on him, he couldn't see it in the clear brown eyes peering back at him. "I asked her to email all of his details to me."

"Good." He wanted to pursue their past, but he'd have plenty of time to broach the subject later. He shut down the computer and put it in the case.

"Can we go now?" Jennie rose and headed for the door. "I really need to get started on those reprints."

He caught up to her. "Any chance I can convince you to lie low?"

She turned and looked at him. "What exactly do you mean by 'lie low'?"

"Once we get to your house, you stay there until we can do a complete threat assessment?"

"Sorry, I can't do that," she said, sounding earnestly apologetic. "I'll barely finish printing pictures on time as it is."

Her answer didn't surprise him. The agency provided security details for a number of people and most of them couldn't just hide out. They had lives to live. Of course, most of them didn't have such an overt threat directed at them. Still, he didn't need to make drastic changes in her schedule. At least, not yet.

"Let me be clear about one thing before we leave, Jen." He stepped in front of her, blocking her exit onto the street. "I'm okay with picking up your negatives and going to the darkroom today, but things will have to change when word gets out that the show is still on."

"And then what?"

"Then whoever trashed this place will try to stop you by whatever means necessary," he answered bluntly. "So we'll need to further restrict your activities."

At his grim tone, some of the color drained from her face, and he saw her clench then release her hands. He hated to be the one renewing her fear, but he couldn't downplay the situation or she might not listen to him when needed.

He escorted her out of the gallery, and once safely in his truck, he focused on making sure no one tailed them. They rode for thirty minutes, the air filled with tension and unease. No matter what he said, it wouldn't change the atmosphere, so he kept quiet and left Jennie alone to peer out the window.

Nearing Beaverton, his phone chimed from the holder on his dash, and she jumped.

"Relax," he said and checked caller ID.

Cole. Good.

Ethan didn't want to share this conversation with Jennie until he knew what Cole had to say, but Oregon's hands-free driving law prohibited any other option, so he clicked his speaker button.

"I'm in the truck with Jennie, and I'm putting you on speaker." He hoped the warning would encourage Cole to filter his words.

"Got an ID on your guy," Cole said. "But you're not gonna like it."

Ethan glanced at Jennie. Saw her eyes narrow.

He didn't want to ask but he had to. "Who is he?"

"His name is Juan Munoz. Lives here in Portland. He's a known member of the Sotos gang."

"What's that?" Jennie asked.

"A local gang affiliated with Eduardo Sotos's drug cartel in Mexico," Cole explained. "They're based out of Matamoros and specialize in exporting cocaine to the U.S."

Jennie gasped.

"This guy is dangerous, bro," Cole went on. "Besides priors for drug trafficking, he's a person of interest in several gang slayings."

A murderer?

Ethan's heart slammed against his chest. He couldn't look at Jennie. She must be terrified. Still, he wouldn't lie and tell her discovering Munoz's history was no big deal.

It *was* a big deal.

Her attacker was wanted in gangland slayings and the important thing to focus on right now was finding out what a vicious killer like Munoz wanted with Jennie.

THREE

Jennie could barely breathe. It seemed as if all the air had been sucked out of the truck.

"I'll get Kat to start tracking down Munoz, but we need to figure out his connection to you," Ethan said. His tone was soft, but did nothing to ease her distress. "I know this is shocking news, Jen, but we need to focus here."

She pulled in a deep breath. Let it go. In, out. In, out. One after another.

"This is crazy," she wheezed. "Just crazy."

"You're right, but dwelling on it won't help us move forward." He paused as if waiting for her to get it together.

She lowered the window to let air fresh from an afternoon shower cool her burning face. Tipping her head toward the opening, she peered at familiar sights as the tires spun over wet pavement toward her home.

She sighed and waited for normal breathing to resume.

"Okay to talk about this now?" Ethan asked.

She nodded.

"So what do you and a Mexican drug cartel or a local gang have in common?"

What, indeed. "The only thing I can think of is that most of the pictures for the show were taken in Mexico."

"What part of Mexico?"

"Just over the South Texas border in Nuevo Progreso."

"Cole said the cartel's home base is in Matamoros. Is that close to Nuevo Progreso?"

"Less than an hour away."

"Then this could be our connection."

"You think I caught a cartel member in a picture?" Her voice was starting to rise again.

"I can't think of any other motive the cartel or this gang might have. I highly doubt they have a grudge against the gallery. And I'm assuming your charity hasn't done anything to anger either of them."

"Of course not. At least, not that I know of."

"So catching them doing something illegal in a picture is a more logical explanation, which means we really need to get those negatives scanned." He glanced at her, and she could see the concern in his eyes, the warmth lingering in the depths.

She may have hurt this man, but she wasn't alone here. He was with her. No matter what they learned next or what happened. He'd stand by her side or in the line of fire until this was resolved.

"Thank you, Ethan," she said. "For being here and not treating me the way I deserve."

He cast a tender glance her way, warming the chill still claiming her body.

She rushed on without thinking it through. "I'm so sorry for hurting you. I didn't want to end things that way, but I…" She couldn't explain so she looked away. There was a pause, then Ethan spoke.

"I told myself this wasn't the right time, but with the way this case is heating up, we need to talk about our past and clear the air before our history gets in the way."

She froze at the tension in his voice.

"I mean," he went on, "we can't just ignore it."

Yes, they could. At least, she had for years whenever thoughts of him had come up.

"Can't we just leave it in the past where it belongs?" She shifted and peered at him. "I'm sorry I even brought it up. It was a long time ago. We're both adults and we can—"

"Can what?" he jumped in. "Spend time together and not remember how much we meant to each other?" He gave her an appraising look. "At least, *you* meant a lot to me."

"Ethan," she said and let her voice fall off before she shared something she'd later regret.

If she shared, he'd look at her with the same loathing she'd seen in her last boyfriend's eyes when she'd told him about her past. Or feel the same judgment people in her church had meted out.

They'd claimed the church was a safe place. A place to cast all of her burdens. When she'd believed them and told them about her pregnancy, they'd judged her and treated her like an outcast—or rather, *more* of an outcast. Her family situation had ensured that she felt out of place even before she shared her secret. She knew her place now and it wasn't with a decent man like Ethan, so why put herself through all of the pain of rehashing the past?

"I'm sorry, Ethan. I just can't talk about it." She clenched her hands and waited for him to yell at her. To get angry. To do anything other than look at her with such intense pain.

He turned his attention back to the road but she couldn't help thinking about his eyes. Those amazing deep brown, almost black eyes.

She'd never seen eyes like his before. Never forgot them. The way they cut through everything. Warming her heart with one look.

She looked away, but could still feel his larger-than-life presence.

He'd always made her feel special. The first man—the only man—ever to make her feel cherished. And here he was. Beside her. The same unwavering set to his prominent jaw, his profile all hard and angular. With this new determination and focus as if nothing could best him anymore.

That was so powerful. And attractive. So attractive. *Jennie, Jennie, Jennie. You have got to get a grip.*

Thinking about him like this was nuts. Just plain nuts. Sure, he'd let go of his professional detachment and gotten personal for a moment. But only because he wanted an answer. Closure, maybe. Nothing had changed. She'd hurt him too badly for him to care about her again.

He pointed out the window. "The one with black shutters yours?" His tone was flat and all business again. The way she wanted it. So why did she suddenly feel sad and alone?

"How did you know my address?" She stared at him.

"I did my homework after Madeline called me." He pulled into the driveway and killed the engine.

Good. She needed to put some space between them. She reached for the door handle.

"Not so fast, Jen. I need to check things out first." His pain vanished and a deadly intensity darkened his eyes to a midnight black, reminding her of where she should focus her mind.

She had no time to linger on thoughts of their past or how he still made her heart beat faster. No time. Not when a killer remained at large and could return any moment to finish what he had started.

Ethan watched a variety of emotions flitter across Jennie's face. She was thinking about Munoz, as was he. But despite the threat, he wanted to move back to their discussion of their past. Have a do-over. This time he'd use more patience and understanding. Not be all blunt and harsh.

He needed to talk about what had happened between them. To get it out in the open so he could let it go, focus on the job and figure out how to keep her safe. But her mind was somewhere else, her eyes staring blankly at his chest.

"Jen," he said, trying to sound detached. "What's going on?"

"Nothing. Really. Just seeing you like this…brings back things I haven't thought about in a long time." There was a tense edge to her voice.

"And from the tone of your voice, I'd say things you don't want to remember."

"It's not that. It's just…" She shook her head as if unwilling to talk about it any more. "Never mind." She grabbed her bag and lifted the handle.

He shot out a hand. "Remember, I go first, Jen. No matter where we are, I always go first."

"Sorry."

He ran around the truck, sweeping the area, keeping his focus on her safety. He escorted her up a damp sidewalk leading to a modest bungalow painted in dark beige. The air smelled fresh. He didn't see any signs of a disturbance…yet.

"My keys," she muttered near the stoop and stopped to dig in her camera bag.

He climbed the steps and found the door cracked open.

"Did you leave this open?" he asked.

"What?" She looked up, her eyes creasing with concern. "No. I mean, I don't think so."

He held out his keys and drew his gun with the other hand. "Go back to the truck while I check this out."

"I probably just forgot to lock it and the wind blew it open."

"What wind, Jen?" He jingled the keys. "I need you to go back to the truck."

She didn't move.

If he was going to get her cooperation now and in the future, he needed to remember she often balked at others telling her what to do. He'd need to dial things back a notch. "Please go to the truck, Jen."

This request seemed to bother her more, but she took the keys and turned to leave.

"Call 9-1-1. Make sure you tell them I was with the bureau and what I'm wearing so some trigger-happy cop doesn't take me out. And lock the doors."

He waited until he heard the lock click then raised his gun and shoved open the door with his shoe, noticing the pry marks on the wooden jamb on the way in.

A forced entry. Just as he'd thought.

He glanced in and out. Caught sight of a family room thoroughly tossed by someone looking for something. Blowing out a breath, he stepped in, picking his way through her personal belongings scattered on the floor and heading toward a doorway. He flattened his back against the wall. Counted to three. Glanced in. A hallway. All clear.

He eased forward, quietly pressing open the first door. Empty and tossed. Obviously Jennie's room, tasteful and understated. Fit her personality perfectly. A quick check of the master bathroom, and back into the hall.

Moving cautiously, he slipped into the main bathroom and slid open the shower curtain. No one. On to the next room. Same story. Set up as a guest bedroom before this creep ripped everything into shreds. Last door, an office, surprisingly neat. Just a few binders tossed on the floor.

On to the trendy kitchen. Interesting. Not touched by the intruder. The garage next. Neat and tidy. He went out the back door. Swept the yard. No one.

Their intruder was gone. Long gone. He lowered his weapon and holstered it as he returned to the living room.

The sofa and cushions lay in tatters, slashed open, the stuffing strewn across the floor. Someone had emptied shelves and tossed every item in the room to the floor like trash. This wasn't some random burglary, but a professional search meant to leave nothing unturned.

Looked as if he entered through the front door, ripped this room apart, then worked his way down the hall just as Ethan had. Stopping his search after the office likely meant he'd found what he'd been looking for in there.

He retraced his steps to the end of the hall and took a closer look. The desk remained intact, bookshelves lined with binders all neatly labeled on the spines stood untouched. He grabbed a binder with this year's date and the word *Chicago* on the outside. Inside, he found three-ring protector sheets filled with negatives.

So this was how she stored negatives.

Empty slots on the shelf could mean the intruder was after negatives. Probably the negatives Jennie had come home to retrieve. Added credence to his theory. This guy didn't want Jennie's photos displayed in public, and these incidents were all about the pictures. But why? That was the question needing answers right now.

Sirens spiraled through the air and Ethan went to meet the police. Jennie, still in the truck as instructed, craned her neck to see him. He wasn't pushing his luck that she'd sit idly by and wait for him to cross the yard, so he picked up speed. She didn't disappoint but whipped opened the door and stood on the running board, peering over the top.

"Is everything okay?" she called out, her voice holding a good measure of concern.

He jogged to the truck before she jumped down and tried to make her way to the house. "There's no one inside now, but someone's been here."

"How can you tell?"

"I'm sorry, Jen, but your place has been thoroughly trashed."

"What do you mean, 'trashed'?" She jumped down as if intending to rush inside.

"Hold up." He blocked her way. "We need to wait for the police to check it out before you go in." Technically not true, but he wanted her to get used to the idea of someone vandalizing her house before actually seeing the mess.

She placed her palms flat against his chest and pressed. "It's my house. I need to see what they did."

Her touch felt hot. He stepped back. If he was going to keep her safe, he had to get a grip and not react to a simple touch.

"Ethan? Is there something else you're not telling me?"

Yeah, you broke my heart and it's never recovered.

He shook his head. "They'll want to collect evidence, and we don't want to contaminate things."

"But *you* went in."

"Because I wanted to make sure we weren't at risk from a panicked intruder. Now that I know you're not in any immediate danger, we should sit tight."

"Should or have to?"

He groaned in frustration. "Is this how we're gonna play things, Jen? I suggest something and you balk at it every time?"

"I just want to see what they did to my house. That's all."

"I'm not trying to boss you around for the fun of it. All of my directives are meant to keep you safe." And to minimize her pain—not that he'd mention that part.

"I appreciate your help, Ethan. Really I do. And I'll try not to argue. I've just been in charge of my own life for so long, I guess I don't take direction well." She stared up at him with wounded eyes he remembered so well.

He fisted his hands to keep from reaching for her. She'd made it clear she wouldn't welcome his touch.

A police car flew down the street, drawing her attention as it screeched to a stop.

"We'll wait here until the officers give us the all clear," he said.

"Can you at least tell me if you have any idea why someone trashed my place?"

"Looks like they took the negatives for the show." He waited for her to gasp or get upset about the loss.

Instead, her expression turned thoughtful, and she glanced at her watch. "It's too late today, but first thing in the morning we'll have to go to the bank and re-trieve my other set of negatives."

"What?" His voice shot up in surprise.

"I always make a duplicate copy of the negatives for my shows. I store them in a safe-deposit box in case of fire." She smiled again. "Good thing I'm so paranoid or I wouldn't be able to reprint the pictures."

This was a good thing? Not in his mind.

If his theory continued to hold water, these thugs would keep coming after her until they were certain she couldn't reproduce the photos again. And maybe they wouldn't stop even then.

FOUR

No matter Jennie's desire to see her house, Ethan shouldn't have let her in. Her private sanctuary had been violated. Rudely violated. Now she stood in the middle of her living room, fear stark and vivid in her eyes again.

He wanted to slip an arm around her shoulders and escort her from the trashed house to a safe location. Had tried it actually, but she wouldn't budge. She'd hung with the forensics team as they meticulously collected every fiber of evidence. They, too, encouraged her to get out of there.

Did she go? No. She wouldn't hear of leaving them to their job and not questioning every little step they took. He knew there was an element of shock in her behavior, an attempt to find some normality after today's terrifying events.

He benefited from it, though. He witnessed the quality of their investigation. The first officers to arrive on the scene took this break-in coupled with the gallery threat seriously, calling in techies, uniforms and detectives to canvass the neighborhood for witnesses, search the house and yard, and collect items.

If they'd gotten lucky, they'd lifted a latent print and would produce an ID, but Ethan doubted their suspect had been so careless. Still, he'd have his sister Kat keep after her Portland Police Bureau friends to see if any items collected tonight produced a lead.

Right now, he needed to give Cole a heads-up. They were taking no chances. Someone might go after Madeline, too, and Cole was leading her protection detail.

Ethan pressed his brother's speed dial. While waiting for him to answer, he double-checked the new lock the locksmith had just installed on the front door.

"How's it going, bro?" Cole asked.

"We had a break-in at Jennie's house." Ethan explained the situation. "I wanted to let you know to be on your guard."

"Will do." A long yawn filtered through the phone. "Little early for that, isn't it?"

"You're having all the fun. Madeline's detail is downright boring."

"This guy might be coming your way so keep your eyes open."

"I will. For the next hour, anyway. I've arranged for Derrick to spell me tonight so I can get some sleep and come back first thing in the morning." As the youngest brother of the family, Derrick embraced all assignments, as did his twin, Dani, so they generally got stuck with the worst shifts—if, in Dani's case, they were given shifts at all.

"Do you think we don't let Kat and Dani in on the action enough because they're women?" Ethan asked.

"Where's that coming from?"

"Kat commented on it this morning when I made assignments for this case."

"I don't know, man. I've never thought about it, but I guess it's possible."

"So maybe you can ask Dani to take a shift, too?"

"What about Kat?"

"I'm taking Jennie to Kat's house to spend the night." He looked at Jennie again and imagined the challenge of convincing her to stay with Kat. "At least, that's what I hope will happen."

"You having trouble over there, bro?"

"Nothing to worry about. I can handle it." Ethan said goodbye and hung up before his perceptive brother probed deeper.

"Okay, miss." The slender man heading up the forensics team stood. "We're finished here."

"So I can clean up now?" she asked.

"Yeah." He slid a finger through residual black powder from fingerprinting work. "Sorry about the extra mess." He lifted his case, the weight pulling down his slight shoulders, and headed out the door.

Jennie looked around the room as if not sure what to do.

"You should pack a bag, Jen. You can't stay here tonight." Ethan gestured at the mess surrounding them for emphasis.

"I won't let them run me out of my own house." She crossed her arms and straightened her shoulders.

"I can't let you stay here."

"They got what they came for. There's no reason for them to come back."

"But you don't know that for sure. The guy came for you on the train. Since he didn't get what he wanted, he'll probably come back." He went closer, softened his tone. "You can stay with Kat tonight, and then we'll figure out a more permanent solution tomorrow."

"Your sister? She doesn't need me hanging around her place."

"She'll be happy to have the company."

"I don't know, Ethan. I mean, I hardly know her."

"I'd suggest you stay with a friend, but you really don't want to bring someone else into this mess, do you?"

"Isn't that what we'd be doing with Kat?"

"She's part of the team and trained to handle something like this."

"Still, I don't want to impose on her." Jennie looked around, and her shoulders sagged a bit. "I'll go to a hotel."

"Hotel logistics make it harder for me to keep you safe. It would easier if you stayed with Kat."

"I don't know."

He had to appeal to something she wanted enough to be willing to inconvenience Kat. "If you stay at Kat's house, she can run your protection detail for the night."

Her eyes brightened. "Really? You'd go home?"

He didn't think she'd jump on this so enthusiastically. It made his gut hurt again. More than a little. "Yes. Kat is quite capable of keeping you safe for the night."

"Okay."

"Great. Go pack a few things and we'll get out of here."

She turned without a word and left the room.

When she was out of earshot, he hissed out his frustration. Was it always going to be like this? So different from the past, when he'd believed they knew exactly what the other was thinking and feeling without asking. Until the end.

"Women," he mumbled and texted Kat, another woman who often pushed his buttons. Normally he'd call her and ask if she'd let Jennie stay with her, but as soon as his sister realized their client was his old girlfriend, she'd hound him about how he felt.

When Jennie bailed, Kat had been there for him and helped him heal. They were still close. More alike than any of the other siblings, they often worked through problems together.

He heard wheels rolling down the hallway's wood floor, and he went to meet Jennie.

"I want to check my email before we leave." She left her suitcase and headed for her office.

He'd rather they get out of here, but she should have received the email from her warehouse manager by now. It would be smart to get someone started on investigating the tattoo connection as soon as possible.

He joined her, leaning on the doorjamb and waiting. She clicked away on her laptop, her face intent and the horror of the day lingering in her eyes.

The printer whirred to life on the credenza, spitting out paper. She retrieved and handed him multiple pages. "This is all the information my manager has on Javier Caldera. In her email, she said again what a great employee he is. He's always asking how things are done and trying to learn as much as he can about the charity." She sounded as if she thought these were good things.

Not Ethan. He saw it as the guy asking too many questions to find a vulnerability in the organization so he could exploit it, but he'd hold his tongue until he had proof to confirm his theory. "I'll pass this on to my colleague in Texas and have him follow up."

"I need him to be discreet. I don't want the agency to get into trouble for sharing this." She closed her computer and put it into a protective sleeve.

"Don't worry, Jen. Patrick is a professional investigator." He folded the email and stuffed it in his back pocket. "C'mon. We should get going."

She hesitated as if her feet were planted to the floor. He cupped her elbow and directed her out of the room before she came up with another reason to stay. She sighed, and he walked behind her, keeping quiet, though he wanted to talk with her about the lingering fear he caught on her face. Simple, plain talk, without dancing around their past as they'd done all day. To help her come to grips with the threat to her life.

But there was no point. She wouldn't let him help. Never had. She'd always been too proud to accept any help. When they'd been together, he'd worked hard to get her to open up. She'd shared very little about her past, so he'd never understood her reasoning. And now, even when she needed a friend the most, nothing had changed. Even if a killer had her in his sights, she wasn't going to let him in.

Jennie used the final minutes of their drive to Kat's house to watch the scenery pass by and to breathe. To focus. To center herself and find some semblance of calm. So what if the guy who stalked her this afternoon was a killer? So what if he'd trashed her house, making her feel unsafe in the place that had always been her haven? She had capable men and women surrounding her and this Munoz guy didn't know she intended to go through with the show yet. So for now, she was safe.

They turned into the affluent West Hills of Portland and climbed high above the city twinkling with white lights. This area of town was foreign to Jennie, though she knew its reputation. It had the same wealth and trappings as many prestigious neighborhoods in the country, just not the formal dress code. Gore-Tex was more common here than cashmere, but the narrow streets they wound through still reeked of money.

Ethan pulled to a stop in front of a fifties-style home

in Forest Park. Jennie clutched her camera like a life-line and waited until he got her suitcase from the jump seat and signaled it was okay to get out.

He came around the front of his truck and opened her door. Earlier he'd put on a scarred leather jacket that, even as worn as it appeared, smacked of money and privilege so fitting for this neighborhood. She didn't know if he'd wanted to cover his bloody shirt or if he was reacting to the falling temperature. She also didn't know if he'd ever tended to his injuries.

"How's your arm?" She hopped down and caught a whiff of his musky aftershave on the evening breeze.

"It's just a scratch." He gestured toward the walk-way.

"I wish you'd have someone look at it."

"It's fine." His gaze moved in sweeping arcs over the area, avoiding her concern.

She let the subject drop, and before they could reach the entrance, Kat opened the door. She was smiling as she stepped forward, but her mouth quickly formed an O of surprise. She stared at Jennie, and Jennie re-turned the favor, taking in Kat's high cheekbones, glossy shoulder-length hair and bright blue eyes.

"You're *that* Jennie." She socked Ethan's shoulder. "You should've told me."

"Can we come in?" Ethan ignored his sister as he pushed past her.

"Welcome, Jennie. It's been a long time." Kat stepped back so Jennie could enter.

"I'm surprised you remember me." Jennie moved

into the open foyer with stairs straight ahead, a dining room on one side, and living room on the other.

Kat closed the door. "Are you kidding? Ethan moped over you for years."

"Enough, Kat," Ethan warned.

"What? You haven't told her, huh?"

"Told me what?"

"I said, enough, Kat." Anger pierced his words.

Jennie expected his tone to hurt Kat, but she seemed unaffected.

"Any word on the picture I emailed earlier?" he asked, setting Jennie's suitcase at the bottom of the stairs.

Kat smirked. Jennie remembered how close the two of them were and how easily Kat saw right through him as she seemed to be doing now. She simply stood and watched him until he faced her again.

"I'm not going there, Kat," he warned. "Just tell me what you found out."

She didn't speak, as if she wanted to push the subject Ethan avoided.

"C'mon, Kat, just answer my question," Ethan said, his tone brooking no argument. "Jennie's had a tough day, and I need to get out of here so she can get some sleep."

"Fine. Narcotics confirmed the tattoo is the Sotos gang's mark. Also, after Cole gave me Munoz's name, I called the detective in charge of the gallery break-in and passed the information on. He'll issue an alert for Munoz and bring him in for questioning."

"I don't suppose they'll let you be present for the questioning." Ethan's phone rang, interrupting the conversation. He dug it out and looked at it. "It's Cole." He clicked Talk.

Jennie could hear Cole's deep baritone rattle something off before Ethan could say anything.

"Slow down, bro," Ethan said and listened.

"Can't you just tell me what it is?" He looked at Jennie, and the darkening of his expression told her something was wrong again.

"I'll call you back after we see it." He disconnected and turned to Kat. "Can we use your computer? Cole's texting a link for an interview Madeline's assistant did with the newspaper today. He says we need to read it."

"This way." Kat headed into the dining room and through her kitchen boasting avocado-green appliances.

Ethan's phone chimed a text just as they entered a bedroom furnished with floor-to-ceiling shelves and a large antique desk jutting from a wall like an island.

Kat had taken her place behind a flat-screen monitor.

"Here's the address." Ethan moved next to his sister and set his phone on the desk.

As Kat typed in the URL, Jennie joined Ethan. She instantly felt the tension radiating off him like heat from the sun. The news clearly would not be good.

She watched as the webpage opened and the headline came into focus. Her heart started to pick up speed.

Local Photographer Not Afraid of Thugs. Show Will Open as Scheduled.

She gasped.

"I second that," Kat said.

Jennie forced herself to read the article adjoining her official head shot, photos of the trashed gallery and a picture of crime-scene tape strung around her house. Linda Becker, the gallery assistant, had told the reporter all about both break-ins. She extolled Jennie's professionalism, said she kept a spare set of negatives and announced that the show would proceed as planned.

Jennie couldn't pull her eyes from the screen.

Oh, Lord, how could You let this happen?

"How did they get this on here so fast?" Kat asked.

"Madeline's assistant already had an interview scheduled today for a PR piece," Jennie answered. "All she had to do was call with an update."

"So much for keeping a low profile," Kat mumbled.

"You think?" Ethan slammed a fist onto the desk, making Kat and Jennie both jump. "I was standing right there when Madeline warned Linda not to tell anyone. She knew better than this. She might as well have painted a bull's-eye on Jennie's back."

Distress brought a lump to Jennie's throat. "Why would she do this?"

"I don't know, but I intend to find out." He stormed around the desk and out the door.

Jennie charged after him, hearing Kat's footfalls

not far behind. By the time Jennie caught up to him, he was in the foyer, talking on his phone.

"I don't care how you do it, Cole," he barked. "I want to talk to Madeline's assistant. Have her at the gallery by the time I get there."

He clapped his phone closed and jerked open the door.

"Ethan, wait." Jennie rushed forward. "I want to go with you."

He turned, his eyes all hard and angry but softening a touch when they met hers. "It's better for you to stay here."

"But I—"

"Please, Jen." His anger faded more, and he sighed out a long breath. "You're safe here. Taking you to the gallery would just invite danger." He looked at Kat. "I'm certain no one knows Jen is here, but don't take any chances. Lock up and stay alert."

With a final glance at Jennie, Ethan left. She felt his loss the moment the door closed. All day she'd wanted him gone. Wanted to be anywhere but with him, and now she wanted nothing more than to see his caring face looking at her. To hear him tell her everything would be okay even though she knew in her heart things had just gone wrong. Very wrong.

"Ethan, wait," Kat called from behind as he jogged down the sidewalk.

He stopped to allow her to catch up.

"Are you going to talk to Jennie?" Kat asked.

"I don't have time for this, Kat." He turned away.

She grabbed his arm. "It'll take a while for Cole to bring in the assistant."

"Then I'll help him."

"You're making a big mistake in running from Jennie with so much unresolved between you. It could jeopardize both of your lives."

"Really?" He studied her. "Suppose you enlighten me on that."

"You're wound as tight as a clock. If you let this fester between the two of you, it might cloud your vision and get in the way of your job. You have to clear the air."

"So what do you propose I say to her, then?" he asked, hating how his sarcastic tone made her tense up. "That after she bailed on me I spent every free minute for a year trying to find her? How about that I turned over every rock in Seaside and every other place she'd lived until I tracked her down like some lovesick weirdo? Or maybe that I found her father and uncovered the past she'd tried so hard to avoid telling me about?" He'd tried to keep his tone free from self-disgust but it filled his words. He was still ashamed of how pushy he'd been, how he'd refused to back down until he'd forced to light things Jennie had had every right to keep hidden. Only then had he learned his lesson and backed off…but not before learning one thing he'd never wanted to know. "No matter what I say, I'll come off looking like a loser."

Kat placed a hand on his shoulder. "It wasn't like that and you know it. You just needed some closure."

"Well, I got it all right, didn't I?" He looked up at the clouds and remembered the pain of finding out the woman he'd loved could replace him in less than a year. "I could've lived without finding out she'd taken off for Texas with that guy."

"It helped you move on."

"I appreciate your concern, Kit Kat. I really do." He squeezed her hand then gently removed it. "But getting to the bottom of the threat against Jennie has to come first. When the time is right, I'll talk to her. Okay?"

"Okay."

Hoping the time was never right, he hugged his sister and headed for his car, feeling her appraising eyes on him even after he drove off.

On the short drive, he tried to think of anything but the hopelessness he'd felt after Jennie had taken off. He'd been desperate to find out why she'd really left. At first, he'd thought it'd be easy to find her. Seaside wasn't that big of a city. But she'd moved and he'd had to go all the way back to her high-school records to track down her father. He'd learned so much about her past and even discovered that she'd given up a baby for adoption.

Surprising, shocking actually, but he saw God's hand in this. He'd never believed his birth mother had loved him. If she had, why give him away? Through Jennie's selfless actions with her daughter, he finally believed his birth mother could've given him up *be-*

cause she loved him and wanted a better life for him than she could provide. So he'd sought her out and found a very similar story. Now they had a strong relationship and it was all thanks to Jennie. But his shame from digging into Jennie's past wouldn't let him tell her about it.

He parked in front of the gallery and pounded on the door. Cole headed down the long, narrow space, now free from debris. Ethan wasn't surprised to see the gallery floor already cleaned up. Madeline didn't let anything get in the way of what she wanted, and she wanted Jennie's show to open on Friday.

Cole unlocked the door.

"She here like I asked?" Ethan pushed past Cole, who snagged Ethan's arm.

"Hold up, bro." Cole stood firm. "Don't rush in there in this mood. Take a minute to cool off first."

Cole was right. Ethan needed to catch his breath. He pulled the email about the warehouse manager from his pocket and handed it to his brother. He explained the tattoo connection and Caldera's position at the Photos of Hope warehouse in Texas. "I'd like you to call Patrick and get him to work on this. Have him report back to you, and you can keep us updated."

Cole's eyebrow rose.

"What?" Ethan asked.

"What happened to *would you* do this?"

"Sorry." Ethan rubbed neck muscles as hard as rocks. "Something about this case is getting to me."

"Something or someone?"

"What's that supposed to mean?"

"Kat told me our client is the infamous Jennie who bailed on you."

"Does no one in this family ever mind their own business?" Ethan scowled at his brother and headed toward the back of the gallery.

He could feel Cole's eyes burning into his back. Too bad his brother chose this topic to take an interest in. Since he'd come home from a second tour in Iraq, he'd rarely gotten involved in anything personal, and Ethan hated to shut him down.

Fresh paint fumes caught his attention and he noticed a new coat of paint covering the ominous message. Good. He'd rather not see the threat again. He found Madeline and Linda in the refreshment area. Madeline stared down on Linda, who was sitting in a wrought-iron chair and fidgeting with the cuff of her jacket.

As he neared, Madeline looked up. "Ethan, good. Now we'll get to the bottom of this."

She moved her focus back to her assistant. Working hard to keep his anger over Linda's betrayal from his face, he nodded a greeting and waited for Cole to settle. He leaned against the wall, his ankles crossed in a casual pose, but Ethan saw the intensity in his brother's eyes. Intensity constantly present since his return from Iraq. Linda cast him a wary gaze, so Ethan sat next to her, drawing her attention.

He kept his posture relaxed and leaned toward her. "Why don't you tell me why you contacted the newspaper?"

"It's my job." She met his gaze with a hard stare, but her hands trembled, making him think she was hiding something.

"Explain."

"I'm in charge of PR. After all the news stories ran about the break-in, I knew people would assume we'd canceled the event and no one would show up. If we don't get a good crowd at an event, Madeline blames me."

He ignored her jab at Madeline. "Do you routinely make this kind of decision?"

"Depends on the event."

She was stonewalling him and his anger was starting to bubble up again. "But for this event you had the freedom to make all the PR decisions?"

"Yes."

Madeline took a step closer and her painted-on eyebrows rose. "You knew I didn't want the press to know about our plans."

"No, I didn't." Linda looked away, but Ethan caught a flash of guilt in her eyes before she turned.

She was hiding something, but what? Had she decided to leak the info about Jennie to the newspaper on her own or had someone coerced her into doing it? Or did she simply not like working for Madeline and wanted to cause trouble?

Madeline circled the table and got in Linda's face.

"Don't lie to me, Linda. I told you our plan was to keep publicity to a minimum and just call the invited patrons."

"I—"

"Don't lie again and say you didn't know that."

Linda crossed her arms and glared at Madeline.

Ethan was more certain she was concealing something, but he still didn't know what, so he merely kept a curious gaze trained on her and waited for her to speak. People often talked during prolonged silences, revealing something they didn't plan to say, just to cut the tension.

His phone rang, and he glanced at the caller ID. Jennie.

"Excuse me." He moved away for privacy. "Everything okay?"

"Fine. I just wanted to see if you were done talking to Linda."

He sighed out a breath. "Not yet."

"But you think she'll tell you something to help us find this creep, right?" she asked, hope blossoming in her tone.

He heard Madeline's raised voice in the background, threatening to fire Linda if she didn't come clean. He glanced back at them. Linda still had her arms crossed and glared up at her boss, defiance now mixed with anger. Even if he kept questioning Linda tonight, he doubted she'd admit her reasons for calling the newspaper, or any connection to the gallery break-in.

They'd need to do some legwork to find out why and how she was involved.

He turned his attention back to the phone. He hated to do it, but he had to tell Jennie that they were no closer to finding and stopping her attacker from coming after her again.

FIVE

Jennie heard a car pull into the driveway, followed by the loud thud of a car door. Had to be Ethan, right on time as promised on the phone last night after he'd told her about Linda's reluctance to cooperate. Just to be sure, Jennie set her coffee cup on the kitchen counter then went through the dining room to the front window to peek out.

Wearing jeans, a clean white shirt and the same leather jacket as last night, Ethan stood next to his truck. Aviator sunglasses hid the direction of his gaze, but he seemed to be staring off into the distance. He'd slipped his jacket back and clamped a hand on his gun; the other hand held a stainless coffee mug. The sunglasses coupled with the gun gave him a dangerous vibe, doing nothing to settle the flutter in her stomach.

He turned as if knowing she watched him, and she let the blinds fall. She returned to the kitchen to clean up breakfast dishes. She was eager to get into the darkroom, but she didn't want to leave a mess behind for Kat to clean up.

She heard the front door open and close.

"Jen?" Ethan called out.

"In the kitchen," she answered and started wiping off the big island.

He entered the room and his presence filled every inch. Calm, confident, alert. All man. And though she'd never admit it to anyone, she was happy to see him. In spite of everything, she felt safer with him.

He slipped his sunglasses into the V of his shirt. "Any coffee left?"

"Some," she said, hating how weak her voice sounded.

He poured coffee into his cup. "You sleep okay last night?"

"The bed in Kat's guest room is very comfortable."

He raised a brow. "Translated, not so good, then."

She shrugged. "I know Kat is capable, but I have to admit, worry kept me awake most of the night."

"Maybe we should talk about canceling the show." He sounded a little too eager for her liking.

"I can't do that."

"Can't or won't?" He stirred cream into his coffee, the dark Columbian blend swirling into a light beige color.

"Won't, I guess."

He sealed his to-go cup then caught her gaze. "Sometimes we have to do things we don't want to do."

"I can't cancel, Ethan." She looked directly into the dark intensity of his eyes to convey her sincerity. "We need those funds. We've already allocated every dollar we expect to earn."

"Don't get me wrong here, Jen. I respect what you're doing with these kids." He paused and set down his cup.

"But?" she asked.

"But if these creeps get to you and God forbid kill you, how will that help the children?"

He was right, but it was a risk she had to take. "If this guy is after me because of one of my photos then canceling the show won't change anything. As long as he thinks there's any chance I still have the picture, he'll be after me. Besides, if I backed down every time I faced danger, I'd never take another picture."

"I don't understand." He leaned back against the counter, his ankles crossed, his hands gripping the edge.

"The neighborhoods these kids live in aren't exactly safe."

"And you go there by yourself?" A hint of disapproval tinted his eyes.

"Yes." He opened his mouth and she held up a hand. "Hear me out before you say anything. I take precautions. I try to arrive early in the morning while the criminal element is still sleeping and the kids are usually outside playing."

·"Why not bring someone with you?"

"I get more natural shots when I'm alone and there aren't people distracting the children."

"Still. You can't go in there unprotected."

"I don't always. Where the law allows, I carry a gun."

"You what?" His tone shot up.

"Why's that so upsetting? I've had ample training on how to fire a gun and the safety procedures for owning one."

He rubbed a hand across his face. "I'm not sure how I feel about this."

She arched an eyebrow and waited until he met her gaze again. "Even if you don't like it, it's what I need to do to stay safe in these areas. And, no offense, Ethan, but it's really none of your business."

He pushed off the counter and paced, his hands fisted at his sides. She didn't like the way this conversation had gone, but he had to know she was in charge of her life and didn't need him to act as her knight in shining armor on a day-to-day basis. Sure, she was thankful for his protection now, but she'd taken care of herself since her mother died and her father made it clear that he had little interest in raising a daughter. If she gave up and let Ethan take over, when he left, it would be hard to go back to her old life.

"We should get going." She went to the sink. "I'll just finish cleaning up and then I'll be ready to leave."

She washed the last of the dishes, and when she turned, he stood inches away.

"Promise me something." His dark, earnest eyes held hers, reaching into her thoughts, and she couldn't seem to draw a full breath.

"What?" she managed to whisper out.

"It might be a good idea to carry a gun in the situations you described, but I don't want you carrying until this problem is resolved."

She could tell him her gun sat locked in a gun safe when she wasn't in dangerous neighborhoods, but she wanted to know what was motivating this request. "Why?"

"You may have learned how to handle the weapon, but when people who haven't had law-enforcement training find themselves in life-and-death situations, they don't always make the best decisions." He lifted his hand and tucked a strand of hair behind her ear. "You don't need to take such a big risk with me around. Let me take care of things."

The urge to surrender was unusually strong after all the years of having to look after herself while her father stewed in his own problems. Her past had always made her want to prove she could stand on her own, but with Ethan, it would be so easy to rest her head against his chest and let him take over.

"Jen?" he whispered.

His tender tone almost had her moving closer to him. Probably what he'd counted on when he'd stepped so near. But she couldn't give in. She needed to end this conversation. "I promise."

"Thank you. Even if I'm no longer a law-enforcement officer, I still can't help thinking like one." Looking down on her, he smiled tenderly.

Her heart kicked into high gear. This moment felt more dangerous to her well-being than if a dozen thugs came after her. She took a step to the side, but he moved away.

"Shall we go?" he asked.

Breathing deep to clear out the cobwebs he'd spun around her independence, she went into the dining room and grabbed her gadget bag and purse before heading into the foyer.

He caught up and stepped in front of her. "Me first, remember?"

If he wanted her to remember his instructions in the future, then he shouldn't stand close enough for her to inhale his freshly showered scent and get lost in eyes that seemed to see to her very core.

He slipped on his sunglasses and moved outside, glancing up and down the street before letting her exit.

"Stay by my side while I lock the door." He twisted a key in the lock then escorted her to his truck.

They rode in silence. Not a comfortable quiet. Not like that summer break when they'd driven with the top off his Jeep as mile after mile of beach disappeared while holding hands and just enjoying each other's company. This was an awkward silence filled with questions and no answers.

When he finally swung the truck into a space at the bank parking lot, she wanted to jump out and rush away, but she knew he'd try to stop her. He tossed his sunglasses on the dash then hopped out and met her at her door, seemingly oblivious to her mood. The warm tint to his earlier gaze was long gone, replaced with a hard-as-nails glint, raising her anxiety over walking through the lot.

"Do you really think someone's watching us?" she asked.

"I doubt it, but let's not invite trouble." He took her elbow, directing her toward the door. "Stay close and don't dawdle."

They slipped inside without incident, and she went straight to the fingerprint reader. She pressed her hand against the screen and the gate to the safe-deposit boxes opened. Ethan trailed her into the vault, where she retrieved her box and took it to a private table. She felt his eyes on her every move until he joined her.

"How many negatives can you get in one box?" he asked as if interested in her work.

"I keep the photos for my last three shows in here, so right now I have three boxes." She lifted the lid.

"Maybe you should invest in a good safe for your home, too. That way if a fire broke out here you'd still have a backup."

"I've thought of that, but I've only been in my house for about a year and just haven't gotten around to it."

"I could arrange the installation of a safe for you."

She looked up at him. Why was he offering to help all the time instead of sniping at her for the way she'd ended things?

She didn't want to ask the question and take them back to the personal realm, but she had to know. "Why are you doing this, Ethan?"

"Doing what?"

"After the way we parted, I expected you to be angry at me, but you don't seem angry at all." She held her breath, waiting for him to tell her how much she'd hurt him, but he didn't show any emotions.

"I was furious. For a long time, actually." His tone was matter-of-fact as if he'd distanced himself from any pain. "Not at you, but at whatever it was that made you lie to me instead of letting me help you work through it."

If he yelled at her or even told her how hurt he'd been, she'd know what to say. What to do. But this kindness and consideration were unnerving. The only thing she could think to do was apologize. "I want you to know how sorry I am, Ethan. I was wrong in lying to you and leaving without a good explanation. I hope you'll forgive me for treating you so badly."

"I forgave you a long time ago." He laid a hand over hers and the warmth echoed his gaze.

She shook her head in wonderment.

"What? Don't you believe me?" he asked.

"No… I mean, yes, I believe you. But it's hard for me to imagine. If I were in your situation, I don't think I could do the same thing."

"Sure you could."

"I don't know."

"Maybe you've never been brutally dumped." He paused, and she cringed at his words. "But someone must've hurt you and you forgave them."

Sure, she had. Plenty of times. Forgiving others was

the easy part. Forgiving yourself? That was the hard stuff. And Jennie still believed some things couldn't be forgiven. A daughter, now fourteen, forgiving the woman who gave her up? Maybe impossible.

"Who are you thinking about?" Ethan asked.

"No one."

"C'mon, Jen. It's me. I know when something's bothering you."

Talking about her daughter was off-limits. Better to keep the focus on Ethan. "I'd like to hear how you let this go."

"I see you're still dodging discussions of your past."

"Maybe, but you're avoiding telling me how you did it."

He groaned. "I'm not avoiding anything. You ever hear of a two-way conversation? That's all I'm trying to have."

She just looked at him and waited.

"Fine," he finally said. "It took time. Lots of time. And lots of help from a friend." An easy smile played at the corners of his mouth as if he remembered this friend fondly. "I was hurt and I blamed you for it. Made my life miserable for a long time. Then my friend reminded me that we all make mistakes. We all fall short of God's glory, and who was I to hold your sin against you if I didn't want others to do the same thing to me?"

She should have known God brought him through

this. "You're lucky. Your faith was always so strong. Unfortunately, it isn't that easy for everyone."

"Are you talking about yourself, Jen?"

"No," she said, though she hadn't forgiven herself, either.

"Well, whoever you're thinking about, it's never too late for forgiveness." His words were comforting, but they did little to get rid of her turmoil.

What if this man caught up to her and killed her? If she didn't forgive herself for giving up the baby, she'd carry her guilt to the grave. And if she didn't ever try to find her daughter, she'd never give her child the chance to know her mother if she wanted to. She'd never really thought of it from this angle before, but this wasn't something to discuss with Ethan.

She smiled at him. "I don't know what to say, other than thank you for forgiving me." *And for being the kind of man you've become. One who is willing to help me even after I hurt you.*

"You're welcome." He squeezed her hand then let go. "Maybe someday we can talk about whoever put that look on your face a few seconds ago, and you can let it go, too."

She dragged her gaze away and focused on loading the negatives into her tote bag. She wanted to tell him about her daughter, but his soft gaze filled an empty hole in her heart, and she didn't want the warmth to go away. The moment she told him about her past, he'd never look at her the same way again.

* * *

Ethan followed Jennie down the sidewalk to the door of the Photo Grotto where she'd be reprinting the photographs. She'd been quiet since their discussion at the bank. They'd stopped by her friend's shop to have the negatives scanned, and she'd barely said a word while she worked. Maybe she was thinking about whatever it was in her past that she couldn't talk about or maybe she was as uneasy about walking down this public sidewalk as was he.

No one had tailed them. He'd remained attentive and focused to make sure of that, but still, his radar beeped at full alert. He had no concrete reason for the feeling, but his intuition rarely led him astray.

"Stay behind me," he said and opened the door to the Grotto.

A caustic smell assaulted his nose as he took in the lobby area filled with displays of every imaginable kind of camera and other items he could only assume photographers used in the darkroom. A cashier's counter ran the width of the room and stood empty.

"That's odd," Jennie said from behind. "Ashley never leaves the front desk."

"Who's Ashley?"

"Daytime receptionist and salesperson. Ashley, are you here?" she yelled and started to move around him.

He stopped her. "This doesn't feel right, Jen. Let me check it out."

"She's probably just in the bathroom."

"Would she leave all this expensive equipment unattended?"

Jennie looked around the room then shook her head. "No. I guess not."

"Wait here." He lifted his gun from the holster and advanced toward the counter, pausing at an open doorway. "What's in there?"

"The darkrooms and a classroom."

He'd check that next, but first he needed to make sure no one was behind the counter. He moved closer and glanced behind it. Spotted movement. He jerked back.

"You're scaring me, Ethan," Jennie said.

He fixed his gun in front, took a deep breath and swung around the counter again.

A young woman lay on the floor, blood oozing from her chest. Likely the missing Ashley. He needed something to stop the bleeding. He searched the room.

"What's wrong?" Jennie asked.

He caught sight of a brightly patterned scarf tied around the handle of her tote bag. "Give me your scarf."

"Why? What's wrong?"

"She's been shot."

"What?" Jennie rushed forward and peered over the counter.

"No!" She fanned her face as if she might faint. "No. Not Ashley."

He locked eyes with her and forced her to focus on him. "I need your scarf to stop the bleeding."

"Yes. Okay." With shaking hands, she untied it from her bag.

Instead of taking it from her, he led her into the space, alternating his gaze between the victim and the hallway leading away from them.

"I need you to take care of Ashley while I see if our shooter is still here."

She stood as if in shock. He gently urged her down to her knees and settled her hand with the scarf over the wound. "Press as hard as you can and don't let up." He made eye contact. "You understand?"

"Yes." Her hand trembled but she kept the scarf in place.

"Is there usually anyone else here at this time of day?"

"I don't know. I'm always at work."

He dug out his phone and pressed 9-1-1 then handed it to her. "Give the operator the details and make sure you tell them we're in the building."

She nodded.

Adrenaline shot through his veins as he jogged to the front door and turned the lock so no one could enter while he checked out the rest of the building. One last glance to make sure Jennie talked with the 9-1-1 operator, and he went to the hallway. Long and narrow, it held three doors on both sides with lights above each one, none of them glowing.

Good, the darkrooms didn't seem to be in use.

At the end, another door. No light. Probably the classroom. He went to the first door. Jerked it wide and whipped around the corner. No one, but everything was trashed like the gallery and Jennie's house.

He moved down the hall. Next room. A mess, but clear. Moving fast, he zigzagged down the narrow space, wrenching open doors to small rooms with photographic equipment and supplies. At each door, his pulse rose, and at the end of the hallway, he took a deep breath. He didn't know what to expect on the other side, and his heart thumped double-time.

Back against the wall, he listened. No sound.

He jerked open the door and charged in. He made a slow sweep with his weapon. A classroom. Chairs lined up. A projector. Back door wide open. Another door leading to the left.

He rushed to it. Ripped it open. The bathroom. Empty. He went to the alley. Glanced out. Back in and out again. Clear. He hissed out a breath and dragged in another. Their shooter was gone.

Sirens wound through the air. A shooting would bring every available officer in the area. Probably an ambulance wail mixed in, too.

He ran back to Jennie. Her eyes were glassy with shock. One hand pressed firmly against Ashley's stomach, the other circling her own waist.

"You okay?" He dropped down next to her, stowing his gun so he didn't draw fire from arriving officers who could mistake him for the intruder.

"No," she answered, her voice not more than a whisper.

Her glazed eyes coupled with her admission weren't

good signs. He hoped the medics hurried. She looked as if she might pass out.

"Let me take over." He reached out.

"No! She's my friend. I'll do this."

"Okay." He backed off, glad her determination still lived underneath the fear. It would help her get through this.

"This isn't a random shooting, is it?" she asked.

"The darkrooms were trashed like someone was looking for something."

"If they read the newspaper article they'd know I have a second set of negatives. I'll bet they thought I stored them here and trashed the place looking for them."

"Likely."

She looked at her friend. "Do you think she's going to die?"

"I hope not."

"I wish we'd warned her. If she dies, it's all my fault."

"You're not to blame in this, Jen." He didn't think she was at fault, but the break-in did have everything to do with her.

This wasn't a burglary gone wrong. They didn't tamper with the register or the expensive easy-to-fence cameras that filled the shelves. This was a targeted attack with higher stakes. Her foe just proved his willingness to kill, and Ethan needed to step up his game to make sure Jennie didn't become the next victim.

SIX

In the Grotto's restroom, Jennie peered at her reflection in the mirror and rubbed her temples, trying to alleviate a headache. The shock of finding Ashley hung in her eyes and left her pale, but at least the panic had receded.

Some, anyway.

She'd cleaned the blood from her hands and arms, but the knees of her favorite jeans were stained. Not that ruining her jeans was important. The paramedics had told Jennie that Ashley needed emergency surgery to save her life. Nothing else mattered right now. Nothing.

Jennie planted her hands on the sink and closed her eyes.

Father, please guide the surgeon's hands and bring Ashley safely through surgery. Heal her and restore her to the happy young woman she used to be before the tragedy. And, Father, please end this whole mess before someone else gets hurt.

Jennie didn't want to leave this room to discover what was waiting for her, but she wouldn't hide out and let others take care of everything. She drew her shoulders back and went into the classroom.

She found Ethan perched on the edge of a table. His back was to her and he talked with Kat, who caught sight of Jennie and lifted a hand in acknowledgment. Ethan jumped to his feet and spun.

"You doing better?" he asked, his gaze softening as he approached her.

"I'm fine."

"You don't look fine, Jen." He reached out as if to touch her, and she took a step back. He let his hand fall, but he looked hurt from her rebuff.

She honestly hated hurting him, but any physical contact with him and the tears she'd fought off for the past hour would flow. "I'll be okay."

"It'll take time to get over this. A shooting will stay with you for the rest of your life." His sympathetic gaze was nearly her undoing so she looked away.

"You're blaming yourself for this, aren't you?" he asked.

"I don't know...maybe. If it weren't for my photos, Ashley wouldn't have been shot."

"You can't hold yourself accountable for what the shooter decided to do."

"He's right, Jennie." Kat came forward. "None of this is your fault. Every bit of the responsibility is on the shooter." She pulled Jennie into a hug and her fruity, fresh scent covered the caustic odors drifting down the hall from the darkrooms.

Jennie let Kat hug her, enjoying the warmth and not

wanting to back off. She could get used to this family surrounding and caring for her. But then what? Return to her solitary existence when this was over? It would be far easier to keep her distance from all of them and stand on her own two feet. She'd made that decision years ago and was still certain it was the right thing to do. The Justices were way out of her league.

She pushed away. "Have we heard anything more about Ashley?"

"Not yet," Kat answered.

"The officer in charge of the investigation promised to call us the minute they know anything," Ethan added, his tone reserved. "Right now we need to move you to a more secure location."

Jennie wondered if she would be safe anywhere, but she had to get out of here. "Where do you want to take me?"

"We'll head to our office for a debriefing and to make a plan. Dani and Cole are waiting in the car." He tipped his head at the back door but never let his eyes stray from her face. "Kat first, then you."

Kat marched across the room, pausing at the door and looking both ways before stepping outside.

"Straight into the car. Okay?" Ethan said, not at all in the bossy tone he'd used yesterday, but with soft encouragement.

Near the door, she remembered her camera and tote bag. "I have to get my things. I left them in the foyer."

"Already in the car," he said.

She nodded and stepped outside. The warm sun

and a tantalizing aroma drifting from a nearby bakery belied the potential danger surrounding them. A cute young woman Jennie recognized as Dani left the idling vehicle while shoving her phone in her pocket. Cole, feet planted wide apart, held his position near the driver's door. Both wore dark glasses, keeping Jennie from making eye contact and offering her thanks.

Kat urged Jennie past Dani and toward the SUV. Jennie waited for Cole to glance at her as she slipped by, but he kept his gaze straight ahead, adding to his bad-boy look that contrasted with Ethan's clean-cut appearance. Cole's hair was lighter and longer than Ethan's, curling over the collar of his denim shirt, and he looked as if he needed a shave.

Jennie climbed into the backseat. Ethan slid in next to her, his eyes watchful. Kat soon slipped in on Jennie's other side and Dani claimed the front passenger seat as Cole took the wheel. These brave men and women silently moving about with confidence and assurance proved they knew what they were doing. She was lucky to have them on her side and was so grateful.

Tears pricked her eyes again. She'd been alone all her life; now she was surrounded by a family. A loving, caring family. If only they could be hers to keep.

Cole headed the car down the alley, and once on the main street, Dani swiveled. "Ethan didn't mention that you were *his* Jennie."

"He didn't tell me, either." Kat gave Ethan a pointed stare. "I had to find out the same way."

"It's not relevant to the job," Ethan ground out between his teeth as if this were the last thing he wanted to discuss.

His sisters shared a knowing look, obviously getting the message to drop the subject. "Derrick called while you were inside," Dani said and pulled out her phone. "He has some news about Linda Becker that he wants to relay."

Eager to hear something that might help them end all of this, Jennie sat forward. "I hope it's good news."

"Could be." Dani turned her attention to dialing and soon put her phone on speaker. "Go ahead, Derrick."

"I've finished my preliminary investigation of the gallery staff. They're all squeaky clean except Madeline's assistant. She has a serious drug problem. Been in and out of rehab since she was a teen. Her finances reflect her struggle. She makes good money at the gallery, but she's swimming in debt. I'm wondering if she was desperate for money and was paid to make that call to the newspaper."

"But why?" Kat asked. "I mean if the point of all of this is to keep the show from opening, announcing it will open as scheduled makes no sense."

"I think it was a knee-jerk reaction by our suspect," Derrick replied. "If he heard the break-in didn't stop the show, he'd need to do something else to scare Jennie."

"And he was probably hoping with a public announcement like this," Dani interrupted as she often did with her twin, "Jennie would think he'd come after her again and she'd run scared, canceling the show before he had to do anything else."

"I suppose that's possible." Kat still looked skeptical.

"We need to interview Linda again," Ethan said.

"No offense, big brother." Kat eyed him up. "But since she shut you and Cole down last night, maybe it would be best to send a woman to talk with her."

"I'll do it," Dani jumped in quickly.

Ethan studied his little sister and seemed to war with a decision. "You'll let us know if anything's out of the ordinary, and if there's any hint of danger, you'll call me."

Dani tensed under his demanding tone, but she nodded.

"Okay, Dani will do the interview." Ethan spoke with authority. "Derrick, how are you coming on vetting the Photos of Hope staff?"

Jennie bristled at the thought that they would investigate the people who worked so hard to help children, but she knew they had to do this, so she didn't comment.

"Nothing remarkable yet. I haven't investigated Caldera since you already asked Patrick to vet him."

"Speaking of Patrick, any word from him?" Ethan asked.

"He's on his way to talk with Caldera right now,"

Cole offered. "I expect to hear something from him this afternoon."

Ethan nodded. "Everything quiet at the gallery, Derrick?"

"Yeah, boring, actually." Jennie could hear the disappointment in his tone.

What was it with law-enforcement types? Always wanting to be in on the action. She'd be perfectly happy to get as far away from this as possible.

"It'll give you plenty of time to keep looking into Linda Becker's background." Derrick didn't argue with his brother, but said goodbye and disconnected.

Ethan settled back, his eyes coming to rest on Jennie. She chose to ignore his questioning look and peered out the window. The photographer in her enjoyed seeing street after street of older homes before they pulled up to a historic brick building with ornate iron scrollwork over the massive oak door. Windows hinted at three floors and the place reminded Jennie of an old apartment building.

She itched to capture on film the way light bounced off the brick, but the moment she stepped out of the SUV, Kat and Ethan rushed her up the stairs and into a large open foyer spanning two floors.

"This way," Kat said and set off down a long hallway.

Jennie and the other Justices followed, passing door after door encased in thick oak molding. At the end of the hall, Kat turned right. Jennie stopped just inside the door to admire the room, and the others slipped past her. The same oak trim circled the ceiling and windows. A large brick fireplace anchored the far corner of the space furnished with a long teak conference table and chairs. Modern artwork hung on the walls, mixed in with a screen and audiovisual equipment.

Ethan set her bags on the table before joining the other Justices in a small kitchenette. Dani flipped a switch on a professional coffee machine and chatted with Ethan. Cole grunted his acknowledgment every now and then, and Kat filled a tray with mugs and a plate of cookies. As a nutty aroma from the pot filled the air, they worked seamlessly together, proving that this day, though terrifying for Jennie, was routine for them. She loved watching them. Seeing their connection. Hearing their concern for each other. Seeing them joke. But she had to remind herself that she wasn't a part of it—and never would be.

As the pot gurgled, Ethan crossed over to her. "You can go ahead and have a seat, Jen."

"This is a fabulous building." Looking around the space to keep her mind off the family who seemed to be worming their way into her heart, she took a chair near the middle of the table.

"Our parents bought it a few years back with the intention of turning it into apartments," Kat said, setting the tray on the table. "We just repurposed it after they—"

A sudden quiet came over the room. She'd have to be blind not to see how much they still missed their adoptive parents.

"We should get started." Ethan pulled out the chair next to Jennie and sat.

Dani and Cole joined them with a steaming coffeepot and sat across the table. Without a word, they started filling mugs and passing them around.

"Before we begin," Cole said as he looked up from pouring and met Jennie's gaze, "if you don't mind my asking, wouldn't it be simpler just to delay the gallery opening until after all this is resolved?"

"How would that stop the guy who's after me? It's the picture he wants, and I'm the one who has it, whether I display it or not."

"True," Cole agreed, "but if you're willing to wait on the exhibit, we can get you out of town to somewhere safe and bring you back to have the exhibit once the situation is under control."

All eyes turned on her. "Madeline's gallery is booked for the rest of the year, so rescheduling— assuming she'd even agree to that—would severely delay raising funds for the kids."

Cole gave her an appraising look. "And that would be worse than being in the sights of a guy who's desperate enough to kill?"

His critical tone had Jennie pulling her shoulders back. "No one is more upset about what happened to Ashley than me, but we need these sales. The money has already been allocated." Her voice broke and she took a moment to look away and stem off tears hovering near the surface since finding Ashley. She spotted a computer and projector. Pictures of the children could better explain what motivated her to continue even after someone had shot Ashley.

She looked at Ethan. "Can I use your projector?"

He arched an eyebrow.

"It will help me explain why I have to go through with this exhibit no matter what."

He nodded, though he seemed hesitant, and went to the computer.

She dug in her gadget bag and pulled out the CD her friend created this morning when he'd scanned her negatives. She handed it to Ethan as he sat down behind the computer. "Select the slide show and start it playing."

He opened the file, punched a few buttons on the projector, and Sonya Estevez's sweet face filled the screen on the far wall.

"This was Sonya. A child who could've benefited from the Photos of Hope program, but her parents were reluctant to participate." Jennie looked around at her audience and saw all eyes riveted to the screen. "She lived in a twelve-by-twelve, one-room house in Mexico. She shared the space with grandparents, parents and four siblings."

The slide changed to Sonya and her family standing proudly outside their patched and dilapidated home.

"There were seven children in the family," Jennie continued, "but two of them died last year from very treatable illnesses." She let this thought age until the next picture displayed the unsanitary pit they used for cooking. "They cook outside, when they have food, and their bathroom is an outhouse."

When the slides advanced and Sonya's face, gaunt from an untreated illness, filled the screen, Dani and Kat gasped.

"This was Sonya a few months ago. Just days before she died from an acute respiratory infection. An infection that was easily treatable." She paused and looked at each person one at a time. "Parents in that part of the country often can't afford proper medical care. They're wary and untrusting of free clinics. Photos of Hope works on educating people like the Esterez family, teaching them that there are ways to treat illnesses like Sonya's. That their children can be saved. But it's slow going. And it costs a lot of money. This is why I can't postpone the show. There will be too many Sonyas in the time it takes to reschedule and raise the money." Tears pooled in her eyes for the loss of the sweet little girl, and she had to look away.

"We've seen enough." Ethan switched off the projector, stood and headed for the door.

Openmouthed, Jennie watched him march out of the room. Was he running away from this? The Ethan she knew wouldn't do something like that, but maybe he'd changed and she didn't know him anymore.

His siblings didn't seem surprised, but Jennie's mouth hung open until moments later when he returned and tossed bulletproof vests on the table.

"We'll be needing these." He gave his brother and sisters each a glance. "Anyone want to argue?"

No one said a word.

"Good, then we'll stop questioning the decision to proceed with the show, and we'll start talking about how to keep Jennie safe." He pulled out Jennie's chair. "Have a seat while we work out the logistics."

His compassion thawed some of the chill from the shooting, and she returned to her chair. They understood the need to move forward. Some of the weight of carrying this burden all alone for so long lifted from her shoulders.

She looked at the vests on the table and couldn't begin to thank them for risking their lives for her. For these children. She wished things were different, but she knew without a doubt that when they finalized this plan and left the safety of their office, they'd all be putting their lives on the line.

Ethan went to the whiteboard and tried to ignore the feelings swimming in his gut, but he failed. Jennie needed to do this. He got it. But he didn't like it. At all. He finally understood that she'd let *nothing* stand in the way of helping these children. She wouldn't back down. That's why he'd had to leave the room for a few minutes.

Sure, he wanted to make a point with the vests, but leaving was more to compose himself than anything else. Letting his emotions get the best of him was a surefire way to get Jennie killed, and that was the last thing he wanted to happen. He needed to focus on logistics and come up with a plan.

"So," he said, looking at the group, "since I know Cole brought you up-to-date on the case this morning, I'd like to get straight to formulating a plan and assigning tasks. Any discussion before we start?"

Murmurs of *no* traveled around the table so Ethan continued. "Our suspect has proven he's desperate to recover Jennie's negatives. We had them scanned this morning so we now have the pictures on CD. I'd like to get started on reviewing them." He wrote *Review Pictures* on the board with a red marker then turned back. "Kat, you know how to work photo software. Is this something you can take on?"

"Absolutely," she answered. "But I'm sure Jennie is better at enhancing digital photos than I am."

Probably so, but he didn't think it was a good idea for Jennie to see these photos in her current frame of mind. "Give it a go," he said to Kat. "Jennie can review the pictures you think are important and add her input."

He didn't wait for agreement, but turned back to the board and wrote Kat's name next to the item then jotted down number two, *Police Follow-Up*.

He turned back to Kat. "Anything new here?"

"No."

"Keep after it." Ethan jotted *Interview Linda* on the board. "I'd like you to conduct the interview this afternoon, Dani."

"No problem for me, if she's available."

"She might be hard to find. Madeline was so miffed at her last night that she fired her." Ethan hadn't shared that fact with Jennie, and a flash of concern lit her face, but he moved ahead, writing *Javier Caldera* on the board and Cole's name next to it. "Let us know as soon as you hear from Patrick."

Cole gave a clipped nod.

"Our last item to review is Jen's schedule for the next few days and to coordinate the security details." He met Jennie's gaze. "The stakes have been raised, Jen, and we'll need to impose those additional restrictions I mentioned yesterday. From this point on, you can have no contact with anyone outside of our agency without our prior approval. No email, no cell-phone use. It's too easy these days to hack into email and trace calls. It probably goes without saying, but you can't tell anyone where you are or who you're staying with."

"In other words, I'm cut off from the outside world," she said, sounding sad.

"Unless we approve. Are you okay with that?"

She nodded.

"Okay, so moving on to printing the pictures for the show. It's obvious you can't go back to the darkroom at the Grotto. Have you thought of an alternative place to do your work?"

"No, but there are several other rental darkrooms in town. I'm sure one of those will do."

"Since our suspect didn't find your negatives, they'll assume you have them and will find another place to work. They'll start with rental darkrooms. We'll need to find a place that isn't open to the public."

"I have friends with darkrooms."

"Friends these men can't easily connect with you?"

She lifted her eyes to the ceiling as if thinking. "There's a guy, Michael. He just moved here a few months ago. I met him at the Grotto, but he's not officially a member of the place, so no one will connect us."

"Good," Ethan said. "Let's take a break so you can call him and then we'll be able to work out logistics."

Jennie nodded and dug out her phone.

"I'd like you to use the landline, please." Ethan slid the agency's telephone toward her.

While she called, Ethan went to Cole, who'd stood and stretched.

"I want you and Derrick to take extra precautions with Madeline. I don't think she's in any direct danger, but these creeps might think they can get to Jennie through her."

"One more concern." Kat approached them. "If they figure out we're providing protection, they'll likely put surveillance on the office. We should avoid bringing Jennie here in the future."

"Agreed." Ethan looked at Jennie and worry gnawed at his gut again.

"You may not know it yet, bro," Cole said, "but you're still interested in her."

Kat nodded. "You could be too close to the situation. We might need to change protective details."

Ethan certainly wasn't on board with that. He watched Jennie as she chatted on the phone. Even after the trauma she'd just experienced, her face was animated and lively. Hard to believe it was just yesterday that Madeline had asked him to take Jennie's protection detail and he'd balked at it. He didn't feel that way today. Not at all. Maybe because he thought he was the best one to protect her. Or maybe Cole was right. Maybe he did still have a thing for her. Maybe.

She hung up the phone and crossed over to them. "Michael said he'd meet us at his house to give us a key whenever we need him to."

"Okay," Ethan said, thankful for the interruption. "Since we're a go on the darkroom, let's get back to work and iron out our details."

Ethan watched Cole and Kat share a knowing look before returning to their seats without further discussion. Still, Ethan knew he should give their suggestion to change details some thought.

He took his place at the head of the table. "Before we get into specifics, Jen, why don't you share any other commitments you have for the next few days that you absolutely can't get out of?"

"I rescheduled everything at work except for a shoot tomorrow morning. I tried to get it reassigned to another photographer, but my boss refused."

"Can't it be postponed?" Ethan asked.

"It's time sensitive. Bitsy Standiford—the woman featured in this article—is receiving an award Friday night for her charitable contributions, and the paper is doing a feature on her for Sunday's edition. So the photos have to be taken this week."

"Why can't another photographer do it?" Cole asked.

"The managing editor promised Bitsy I'd do it. When she saw my photos in the paper for my show, she insisted on having me do the shoot. She's an investor in the newspaper, so he agreed. Supposedly, she thinks my connection to Photos of Hope will make her seem even more giving." Jennie wrinkled her nose as if the thought was distasteful to her.

Ethan's first reaction was to say she couldn't go. On the other hand, if they could do a risk assessment and determine the threat was low, engaging in a normal activity could help remove some of her anxiety. "How many people know about this shoot?"

"My boss and the reporter assigned to the story would be the only ones who need to know."

"Do you go directly to the location or stop in at the paper first?"

"Directly."

"Can you jot down the address and give it to Cole?" She nodded.

He let his gaze connect with Cole's. "You're the best at logistical details. I'd like you to check it out—including a security check on the photographer and editor—and if you think it's safe, plan the transport."

"You got it," Cole answered. "I'm assuming you want me to check out Michael's darkroom first?"

Ethan nodded. "It's also a good idea to avoid Jennie's usual haunts for the next few days." He looked at her again. "And that includes your house. Are you okay with staying at Kat's until the show is over?"

"Yes, if Kat's okay with it."

"Are you kidding?" Kat laughed. "I like having you there."

"Kat also raised a valid point earlier. If our suspect determines we're providing protection it could lead him here. I'd like to hold any future meetings at your place, Kat. Since you've only owned the house for a month, the deed won't be recorded yet and there's no paper trail that will lead them to us."

"Fine with me," Kat said as Cole's phone rang the army's theme song.

He lifted it and looked at caller ID. "It's Patrick." He answered and left the room.

They spent the next twenty minutes discussing transport details from Kat's place to the darkroom. Ethan could easily drive Jennie every day, but he wanted to mix things up so there was no consistent pattern for attack.

He caught Dani's gaze. "If Jennie goes to the shoot tomorrow and if Cole thinks I need assistance for the transport, I'd like your help."

"You got it." Her lips twitched in a brief smile.

Yeah, he was right. They'd kept the sisters away from the danger too long. Time to let them spread their wings so they weren't stifled. He only hoped he could back off and let them do the job.

Cole returned, and Ethan didn't like his scowl.

"What'd you find out?"

"Patrick couldn't find Caldera. He hasn't shown up to work today and seems to be AWOL." Cole dropped onto his chair. "He did learn that Caldera's in the U.S. illegally. He came here two years ago. Until then he was a very active member of the Sotos drug cartel as an enforcer."

Jennie gasped. Her expression said she knew an enforcer employed drastic measures to make sure no one double-crossed the cartel.

"He's also cousin to none other than our Juan Munoz," Cole added.

"So there *is* a connection between them," Ethan said.

"The big questions we need to ask now are," Kat said, then paused as if this needed emphasis, "are Munoz and Caldera working together? Is Sotos the one pulling their strings? And if so, why?"

SEVEN

Ethan ignored the caustic chemical smell saturating Michael's miniscule darkroom as he focused on Jennie. She seemed calm, but was it just a front? Since Cole had shared the news of Caldera's involvement with the cartel, Ethan had been fighting the desire to hold her and comfort her. But with feelings swimming through his gut that had nothing to do with her safety but everything to do with her as a woman, he had no business taking her in his arms. Not when he'd never enter into another relationship with her.

He should just go outside and stand guard, but he didn't want to leave her alone with worried thoughts that traveled across her face like a stock-market ticker ever since they'd heard about Caldera. Even in the space lit only with a soft glow of the red safelight, he could still see her lingering concern. He wanted to tell her everything would be all right, but that was a promise he couldn't make. Besides, she didn't seem to want to talk.

He'd encouraged her by asking open-ended ques-tions, but she'd gone straight to mixing up foul-smell-ing chemicals then pouring them into trays and turning on an exhaust fan, thank goodness. She'd then bent over a large piece of equipment she'd called an enlarger. She slid negatives into some sort of carrier, shone a light down through the negative and played with a bunch of knobs. Now she slipped a piece of paper into another carrier and hit a switch.

She took a step back and looked up at him. "It's hard to do this with you watching me so closely."

"Sorry." He smiled. "This is pretty interesting stuff."

"Honestly? Or are you still trying to figure out how I'm doing with everything that's happened?" She'd always been able to read him.

"You know me too well, don't you?" he answered.

The light went out and she picked up the paper, slid it into the first tray and set a large timer. "So you don't think this is interesting, then?"

"No… I mean, yeah, it's interesting. I had no idea printing a picture involved so many steps."

With a gentle rocking motion, she sent waves of chemicals rushing over the paper, where the first hint of a picture appeared. "Actually, this is the second step in the process. You have to develop the film first."

"And that's done in a darkroom, too?" he asked, hoping to keep her mind occupied.

"Complete darkness. You can't even have the safelight on for the first step." Her voice had taken on an excitement he'd not heard in years. She picked up a small stainless-steel tank, opened it, then lifted out a reel. "With all the lights out, you open the film container and lace the film through this reel. When you're done you seal it in the tank and then you can turn on the lights."

"So you can't see what you're doing?"

"Right. It's all done by feel." She peered down at the paper, now clearly a photo of a little boy, and then, using plastic tongs, she lifted the paper out of the first tray and slid it into the second one.

He imagined her at the Grotto in the inky darkness of a room similar to this one. The door locked by a measly privacy lock set—the easiest of locks to penetrate—that could be opened from the outside by poking something narrow into the opening. Some hulking guy with ulterior motives barging into the room and attacking her.

Not if he could help it.

When this was all over, he'd talk to the owner of the Grotto about safety precautions for their clients. He'd insist on having dead bolts installed on all the doors and making the door to the hallway accessible only with an electronic card or code.

"What's wrong?" she asked him.

"Nothing."

She arched a brow and studied him. "Looks like you're thinking about something pretty serious."

Nothing he'd share. "How in the world did you get started doing this?"

"You say that like it's a freakish thing."

"Not at all." He laughed. "It's just that this involves

lots of equipment and knowledge, so I wondered how you began, that's all."

She eyed him for a few moments then returned her attention to the tray. "When I was in high school, I couldn't afford to go to extracurricular activities. So I joined the yearbook staff and went to the events to take pictures for the yearbook."

"Sounds like a good way to be able to attend."

"Yeah… No…" She shrugged. "I mean, not really. I got to go to everything, but I still wasn't a part of anything."

"I don't follow."

"Even though I was there, I was still invisible. No one talked to me or noticed me. I was still the new kid from the wrong side of the tracks." She shifted the picture to the next tray and moved it around in the liquid with the tongs.

He watched her and waited for her to look up again. He'd always wondered if something in her past was the reason she'd bailed on him. She'd refused to talk about her background when they dated. But now she seemed more open, as if she was ready to have a conversation about her past, and maybe discuss their relationship, too.

As if feeling his eyes on her, she glanced at him. "What?"

"This is the first time you've talked about how you were raised."

She lifted her shoulder in a quick shrug. "It wasn't relevant to any of our discussions."

"Even that last one. When you split."

She stilled her hand midair, but didn't look at him or say a word. He'd hit on a nerve.

"Why'd you really leave me, Jen?" he asked softly to encourage a response.

Quiet descended on them. Like a rough blanket on a sweltering day, it felt oppressive and he needed to end it.

He moved closer, her sweet fragrance overtaking the chemical odor. "Jen?"

She stood with her hand frozen in the air. He eased even closer and she took a hurried breath.

"We need to talk about this," he said.

"I need to focus on what I'm doing here." She lowered a shaking hand, and he heard a breathless quality to her tone. Their closeness was affecting her, too.

She peered at him for a long moment. He stared into the bottomless brown eyes and felt her drawing him in again. Her eyes held so much anguish it made his chest hurt.

"Please, Jen," he said, hoping she'd let down her defenses and talk. "I need answers." He reached for her, intending to pull her into his arms, then remembered why he shouldn't and let his hands fall. "And talking this out will be good for you, too. It'll give us both some needed closure."

She shivered before her eyes cleared, and she

stepped away, taking the photograph to a wire rack. "This isn't a good idea, Ethan. Our past is in the past. Let's just leave it there. We have different goals and dreams, and no matter the obvious attraction between us, we don't need to go there."

He could see her struggling to put the walls back up between them, and that was the last thing he wanted. He crossed the room and turned her by the arm. "Have or had?"

She gave him a narrow-eyed gaze. "Had, I guess. I don't really know much about you now." She freed her arm and turned to the counter. "I need to work."

He let out a long breath. Dragged in another. The room was thick with tension and it felt stifling. When he'd taken this case, he never imagined it'd be like this. He was over her. Had been for a long time. So how could he know every time he looked at her some deep-rooted insecurity would rise up and blindside him like this, making him just as desperate for answers as he'd been all those years before?

He watched her as she repeated the same procedure with another picture. He should call Madeline. Tell her that he'd put one of his siblings on Jennie's detail, that he couldn't do this.

Jennie looked over her shoulder, lingering anxiety darkening her eyes. His heart broke. Shattered into pieces. He took a step back. He had to get away from her. Just had to or he was going to get hurt again.

But he couldn't go. Not now and leave her care to

anyone else. He didn't want to do this, but there was no other choice. He trusted his family, but making sure Jennie stayed safe was more important than his feelings, and he wouldn't back off while her life was in jeopardy.

Jennie kept her back to Ethan. With his restless shifting and sighing for the past few hours, she'd barely been able to work. Since their conversation, he'd moved from sitting on the counter behind her and swinging his legs to either pacing or leaning against the door. She wanted to ask him to leave. To go outside and wait, but if she looked at him again, looked into his eyes that had reflected her feelings, she'd be lost.

"I realize you need to focus, but is any conversation off-limits or just our past?" His words rushed out as if he'd been ready to say this for some time.

Maybe a conversation about some meaningless topic would lighten the tension. "We can talk."

"In all the confusion, I didn't ask if there were people who might be wondering where you are and if we need to contact them so they don't worry about you."

She glanced up at him. "People at work know I'm unavailable."

"Isn't there someone in your personal life you might need to contact?"

She slid a fresh piece of paper into the easel. "My friends are used to me taking off without notice. So they shouldn't miss me for a few days."

"What about a boyfriend?"

Surprise made her hand jerk, and she ruined the photo.

"I'm not seeing anyone."

He pushed off the door and came closer. "Why not? If you don't mind my asking."

"I do mind." Telling him about her almost fiancé, Owen, rejecting her because she couldn't commit to her daughter would bring them right back to the parts of her past she wanted to keep hidden. She needed to put the focus on him. "How about you? Are you dating?"

"No."

"Why not?"

"It's personal."

She pivoted and searched his eyes. "See? When the tables are turned, you're not so happy answering my questions, are you?"

He locked gazes with her for a moment, and she made sure hers held a challenge. His battled back for a few moments, but finally he shook his head.

"Fine," he said. "A few years ago, a woman bailed on me a month before our wedding day."

The air seemed to leave the room, and it felt as if he'd plunged a knife into her back. Shocked at this visceral reaction, she took a step back and busied her hands by moving tongs on the countertop.

What was going on here? She'd long gotten over her feelings for him, hadn't she? If so, why did the thought of him getting married hurt so much? And why, for goodness' sake, did she want to continue this conversation when it could only lead somewhere neither of them seemed to want to go? Because he brought it up and now she needed to know, that's why.

She faced him again. "What happened?"

He shrugged as if it was unimportant, but she could see his lingering pain. She let her nails bite into her palms to keep from moving toward him and comforting him but didn't take her eyes off him as she waited him out.

He ran a hand around the back of his neck. "We wanted different things. Carla loved her job more than anything. She got a promotion and decided her job as a VP didn't mix well with marriage." He didn't say that she'd loved her job more than she'd loved him, but Jennie could hear the hurt in his tone that said he couldn't believe the woman he'd planned to spend his life with chose a job over him.

The light went out behind her and Jennie dragged her gaze away before she got caught up in his anguish and did something dumb like rest a hand on his shoulder and tell him that she hated that he was hurting.

She took a few deep breaths and slid the paper into the developer. "And you haven't dated since then?"

"No." Jennie never knew one word could hold so much sadness.

"Why not?" As much as she wanted to look at him, she kept her eyes forward.

"You can only be abandoned so many times in life and be willing to put yourself out there again." He moved next to her, and she looked up at him, trying to hide the sorrow, maybe guilt, for her part in hurting him.

He peered over her head, a distant look in his eyes. "For as long as I can remember, I felt different from my friends. I didn't know why until I finally realized that my parents—the people who were supposed to love me unconditionally—chose to give me away." He shrugged. "I wanted anything back then but to be different. I'm okay with it now, but when someone walks out on you, it all comes back."

Jennie knew exactly where his sadness was coming from. Had lived it herself. Her mother dying. Her father leaving her emotionally. Her church friends and Owen rejecting her when they learned about the baby. And she was the worst one of all, abandoning her own child and then, when she was afraid to tell Ethan about it, abandoning him, as well. She couldn't continue with this discussion.

"I think we should move on," she said and went back to work.

"Now you're mad."

"I'm not mad, Ethan."

"Then what?"

"It's nothing. I just need to work." She continued moving the photo through the trays, one by one.

She could feel his intense gaze, but he didn't say anything else. She was glad he didn't push harder. Spending time with him brought back the reasons she'd fallen in love with him the first time. If she were willing to consider a relationship with any man, Ethan could be a contender.

But nothing had changed. Too much stood between them, too many shadows in her past that made her all wrong for him. They could never get together again, never, and that thought made her sad. Sadder than she'd been in a very long time.

EIGHT

Ethan felt wrung out. He couldn't have been happier when Jennie finally finished her darkroom work for the night and they headed back to Kat's house. Jennie's expression had turned so soft in the darkroom that he'd had to cross his arms and keep them crossed to stop from reaching out and holding her.

He wanted to put space between them, but Kat ended that wish the minute they walked in the door. She called to them from the dining room, urging them to look at photos on her laptop. Now he stared over her shoulder, as Jennie stood closer to him than was good for his warring emotions. It was beyond him how he could still be so attracted to her when she worked so hard to keep him at a distance.

Maybe he was just drawn to women who weren't good for him. Carla was a perfect example of that. Deep down, he'd known her job was far more important to her than their relationship. So why had he stayed with her and then asked her to marry him?

"I've only gotten through the first disc, Jennie." Kat nudged Ethan and gave him a pointed look urging him to pay attention. "But these five photos deserve further scrutiny." She opened each picture side by side as large thumbnails. "So these were all taken in Mexico?"

"Yes."

"Were these pictures supposed to be in the show?" Ethan shifted away from Jennie so her bottomless brown eyes weren't so close and drawing him in deeper.

She pointed at the screen. "Only this one."

"So this might be the photo they're looking for," Kat said. "The big question is, why?"

Ethan studied the screen. "There are people in the background standing by that car. Any way to enhance it more?"

"I can work on it," Jennie offered. "But I have to tell you, I usually shoot with a shallow depth of field, so we may never be able to clearly see the background."

"Explain," Ethan said.

"When I take pictures, I want the children to be the main focus. So I adjust the settings on my camera to center on the child and blur the background. I only keep the background in focus if it enhances the child's plight."

"Such as?"

"Remember the photos I showed you of Sonya's family? I wanted you to be able to see the house, so I made sure the people and the house were both in focus."

"So this might not just be about people you captured but there could be something in the setting, as well?" Ethan asked.

"Yeah, I suppose."

"I have to admit, I was mostly looking for people," Kat said. "We'll need to go back through the CD." She saved the photo on her computer and ejected the CD. "I'll review these on my office computer if you want to work on enhancing this one, Jennie."

"Sure," Jennie jumped in quickly.

Too quickly for Ethan, as if she was trying to get away from him as fast as possible.

She sat and tugged on the neck opening of the Kevlar vest he'd asked her to wear during transport since the shooting. "Can I take this vest off now?"

"Sure. You only need to wear it in transport."

She pulled the Velcro straps, slipping out if it as he did the same with his.

"Since you're the only one without a task, brother dear, can you order dinner?" Kat looked at him with an impish grin so reminiscent of the sweet little smiles from her childhood.

He chuckled over the joy she took in giving him a menial task and hung his vest over a chair. "Is Chinese all right?"

"Sounds good to me," she called on her way out of the room. "I'll take my usual."

"You still like orange chicken?" he asked Jennie.

Her head lifted, surprise lighting her eyes. "You remember that?"

"I remember everything, Jen." He held her gaze, which said she remembered, too.

"It's still my favorite," she said softly and faced the computer.

"Then that's what I'll order for you." He waited for an acknowledgment, but she stared ahead. "I'll be in the living room if you need me," he said and left the room.

He placed the order for delivery from their favorite Chinese restaurant and settled onto the sofa where he could keep an eye on the front door. He opened a browser on his phone and typed in *Sotos Cartel*. The search engine returned pages of entries. He spent the next thirty minutes reading details of murderous rampages that made his stomach churn. He studied all the photos of the cartel members in case he encountered one of them in Jennie's files.

Finally, he entered Eduardo Sotos's full name into the search box. An article denoting the Drug Enforcement Administration's ten most wanted criminals caught his interest. He clicked the DEA link and let out a low whistle. Sotos's name held the number two spot. This creep was a killer of the highest caliber.

The doorbell rang and Ethan jumped.

"Relax," he whispered to himself as he went to look through the peephole.

The moment he opened the door, the tasty aroma of their food helped eliminate his sour stomach from the internet research. He tipped the delivery guy, took the bags into the dining room and set them on the table near Jennie. She didn't even look up at him. In fact, she didn't seem to notice he'd come into the room.

That was good for his ego.

He went through the kitchen and down the hall to Kat's office.

"Dinner's here," he said from the door of the small room overflowing with books.

He turned to leave.

"Wait." She looked up, her eyes narrowed. "This is going too slow. If I make a copy of the disc, can you take your laptop to the darkroom tomorrow and look at some of these, too?"

"Sure." He hadn't had to think twice before agreeing. He'd have a good reason to sit outside the darkroom instead of next to Jennie.

Kat stood and came around the desk. "Your research turn up anything of interest on Sotos?"

"He's on the DEA's top ten list."

"Whoa," she said.

"Jennie doesn't need to know about this, so let's keep it between us."

"The more we find out about Sotos, the more worried I get for her."

"As long as we bring our A game, we're able to protect her, Kat." His tone was confident, but the feeling didn't travel to his gut.

"Nice try, brother, but I know you." She slipped her hand into the crook of his arm and started for the door. "You're trying to hide it, but your face holds a healthy dose of concern."

He shrugged and hoped by the time he got back to the dining room he'd manage to put on his game face for Jennie. "There is no better skilled team to protect her than the Justice team. Remember that."

"We *are* the best." She looked up at him. "But even the best sometimes fail."

"Let's not think that way, okay? And especially don't let Jen hear that kind of talk."

"No worries there. I'd never spook a client like that. Just wanted to let you know what I was thinking." She gave him a quick hug. "So let's eat."

She preceded him into the kitchen. Her phone rang and she looked at the display. "The detective in charge of the case."

Ethan hoped this was good news for once. As he gathered plates and utensils, he listened to her side of the conversation. Sounded as if they were talking about Ashley and that she was on the mend from the darkroom shooting. He couldn't wait for Kat to get off the phone and confirm it.

He took the first load of items into the dining room. Jennie didn't move, not even after he let the silverware clang to the table. When he returned to the kitchen for drinks, it sounded as if Kat was ending the conversation.

He took sodas into the dining room and Kat joined them. "Good news, Jennie. Ashley's going to be okay."

Jennie looked up. "Really?"

"Really," Kat answered. "She came through surgery fine and the bullet didn't do any damage they couldn't repair."

Jennie's answering smile was dazzling. She's always been completely unaware of the captivating picture she made, but Ethan didn't miss it. His heart turned over, and he gritted his teeth until he could control the emotions.

"Was she able to identify her attackers or give the police any leads?" he asked Kat.

"Not yet. But they're still working with her, hoping as she regains her strength something will come back to her."

"Make sure you follow up with them."

Kat nodded and turned to Jennie. "Any luck with the picture?"

"It's a little better, but I can't improve it any more."

Ethan moved behind her and looked over her shoulder. Better, but still not clear enough to identify the men in the background.

"Maybe if we talk about the day you shot this, something will come to mind." He handed a plate to Jennie. "Do you remember that day, Jen?"

"Yeah. It was the first time I met Nola."

"I'm amazed you remember all these children by name," Kat said.

Jennie shook her head. "Not all of them. But Nola's name made her stand out. It's short for Manola and means 'God is with us.' I was touched that this family, who had nothing, was sure God was with them and that He'd take care of them."

"So what's her story?" Ethan joined Kat in opening the take-out boxes and releasing a mixture of tangy spices into the air.

Jennie reached for the rice. "I'd gone to Progreso that day. I was on my way out of town and saw Nola sitting on a crumbling wall, her knees tucked under her chin. She was crying. So I went to talk to her."

"I'm guessing that means you speak Spanish," Kat said, scooping a large spoonful of chicken onto her plate.

Jennie nodded. "Nola told me her mother had died a few days ago and she didn't know how her *abuela*— grandmother—was going to take care of them. Her grandmother was crippled and couldn't work."

"What about the father?" Ethan asked.

"Nola said he'd taken off years ago and no one had heard from him."

Kat grabbed a soda and took a seat. "So what did you do?"

"What I always do when I find a child like this. I asked her to take me to see her *abuela*."

"And did she?" Kat asked.

"Yes," Jennie continued. "We walked for a long way along the river dividing the U.S. and Mexico. She and her grandmother live in a tiny run-down shack in the middle of nowhere. Her grandmother was out front sitting in a rickety chair. I explained my program and asked if I could take Nola's picture. That I'd pay her and enroll Nola in a subsidy program. Her grandmother sobbed and thanked God."

"And then you took these photos." Ethan heard the sadness in his own voice. Sadness for the child, but if he was honest the heartbreaking look on Jennie's face made him feel sadder.

"Yes," Jennie said, then forked a wedge of orange chicken in her mouth.

"Anything unusual happen?" Ethan asked, hating that he had to keep her memories pinned on an event that was obviously painful to her.

"Oh, my gosh." Her fork clanged to the plate. "I can't believe I forgot about this. Where's the disc?"

"In the office," Kat answered.

"Can you please get it?" Her eyes held a glint of determination.

Kat left the room, but Ethan kept his focus on Jennie. He'd always loved seeing her so strong and resolute. Whenever this look captured her face, she achieved whatever goal prompted it.

It reminded him of the day his mother had asked to see Jennie's dress for his parents' anniversary dinner.

Years ago, when she'd stepped into the room, he could only gape at the stunning picture she'd presented. His mother had stared, too, but she didn't think the dress was appropriate, so she'd offered to buy Jennie a new one. They'd argued and Jennie had said she'd either wear her dress or not come to the party. Jennie won.

Kat returned and gave the CD to Jennie. "So what are you looking for?"

Jennie slipped it into the computer. "Two men came

around a fence to get into a car when I was shooting Nola's picture. They caught me by surprise, and I remember lifting the camera while clicking. I know I got a shot of them before they moved out of sight."

"I'd have remembered a car so I'm certain it's not in the pictures I've gone through," Kat said.

Ethan joined Kat behind Jennie and watched as she started scanning through pictures. He heard the back door open and close, and he reached for his gun.

"I hope that's Chinese I smell." Dani's voice came from the kitchen.

Ethan hissed out a breath and smiled at his sister as she entered the room with a plate in hand. "So you want to hear about my little chat with Linda?"

"You know we do," Ethan answered.

Dani spooned rice onto her plate. "After talking to her for a while, she broke down and confessed she was paid to make the call to the newspaper."

"Really?" Jennie peered at Dani over the laptop.

Dani nodded. "She agreed to leak the information to the newspaper in exchange for drugs."

"And did she ID the person who gave her the drugs?" Ethan asked.

"Said she didn't know his name. He was a friend of a friend."

"Then we need to—"

"Interview the friend?" Dani sat down. "Linda's story didn't play with me, so I've already talked to the friend. She claims Linda is lying. She doesn't know any dealers and never hooked Linda up with one."

Ethan sat next to Dani. "You think the friend is on the up-and-up?"

She shrugged and chewed. "Seems like it. More so than Linda, anyway. I can look into her background, but I think we'd be better off tailing Linda to see if she leads us to her connection."

"You volunteering?" Ethan made eye contact with her.

"You know I am." Her eyes held enthusiasm mixed with the rush that came with solving a law-enforcement puzzle.

He hated the idea of letting his kid sister tail someone without backup. Still, he wanted to change his overprotective attitude and was committed to letting her do her job. "Then you've got the assignment. Coordinate with Derrick and Cole to schedule a break."

She gave a quick nod, but as she bent forward to fork up a bite of food, he saw a quick smile tug at her mouth. He turned back to his own food, as did Kat, but Jennie kept working on the computer file. She needed to keep eating. He pushed her plate closer and considered telling her to eat, but she'd likely just balk at his suggestion.

"There," she said and turned the computer to face him. "I'm guessing these are the men we're looking for." There was no mistaking the grim edge to her voice.

Ethan looked at the screen. The child Jennie had told them about sat in the foreground, but off to the side and so ragged and dirty, his heart twisted. He looked beyond her to the men and SUV in the background. Jennie had said they'd be in focus, but they were still too blurry. "Can you improve the focus?"

"Maybe." She turned the laptop and started clicking the mouse. "You should go back to your dinner. This is gonna take a while."

He picked at his food. The photo had taken away what little appetite he'd once had. If Jennie couldn't produce a clear photo tonight, he'd contact his buddy Jack at the FBI. The bureau had state-of-the-art equipment, and if anyone could enhance the photo, they could. Ethan only prayed that these men weren't even more dangerous than the two thugs they'd already identified.

NINE

Jennie softly closed the darkroom door, hoping Ethan wouldn't hear the click. At least today, he'd opted not to join her but had spent all morning sitting outside the door. He'd said it was so he could review more of her photos on his computer, but she got the feeling he was also relieved not to share close quarters with her.

After hours of printing photos, she'd planned to take a break and ask if his FBI contact had made any progress in enhancing the photo from Nola's shoot. Jennie had done more work on the picture last night, but it wasn't clear enough to run through facial-recognition software. So Ethan had emailed it to his friend at the FBI, and she really wanted to know the status. But when she'd peeked out and caught the grim look on his face, she'd decided it wasn't a good time to talk to him. When he heard something, he would tell her.

A quiet knock sounded from the door.

"Jen, did you need something?" Ethan called out.

He'd heard her. Of course he had. He missed nothing. Not the worry eating at her last night, not the anxiety she felt when wearing the bulletproof vest on the ride over here and probably not the way her heart started beating a little bit faster whenever she laid eyes on him.

"Jen?" he asked again.

She opened the door. "I just wanted to ask if you've heard anything from the FBI, but I got one look at your face and decided you might want to be left alone."

"I haven't heard anything yet."

"So why the grim face?"

"These pictures. The condition these children live in is shocking." He shook his head. "I've often wondered if I hadn't been adopted if my life would've been this horrible."

The tone in his voice turned her stomach. She'd grown up in a very similar manner. Okay, maybe not that bad, but squalor, nonetheless. He could never accept her upbringing without pitying her. The last thing she wanted from him was his pity.

The question of the hour was, what did she want from him? Was she hoping for a quick resolution to her problem and then they'd part ways for good, or was she beginning to want more? If so, it really didn't matter. They'd never work as a couple. She just had to remember that.

She'd keep their focus on the pictures. "I hate seeing these children suffering like this, too. But if looking through these pictures can lead to the arrest of whoever's behind this, then it's worth doing."

He watched her and worked the muscles in his jaw.

"What?" she asked.

"Arresting them may not be quite that easy."

"I don't understand."

"If the picture we sent to Jack doesn't show those men doing anything illegal or connect them to the recent events, then it may not be enough hard evidence to make an arrest."

"So how do we get that evidence?"

"Hopefully the fingerprints lifted at the gallery or darkroom will lead us to them."

"And if the prints match the guys in the photo, then can they be arrested?"

"Sure. The police can make an arrest based on prints." He paused and caution flickered in his eyes. "But you have to consider that the guys who are threatening you may not be the guys in the picture. My guess is, the men in the photo are high up in Sotos's organization and that's why they want the pictures. The guys threatening you are just low-level flunkies."

"So you're saying we can't catch the top guys, then?"

"No, I'm not saying that. We have a chance at arresting the men doing the dirty work and getting their confessions, but it will be hard to get anyone in the Sotos organization to roll over on the big guys."

"But not impossible."

"Right. Not impossible."

His tone said he was just humoring her. She was in bigger trouble here than she'd imagined. A chill took hold of her and she shivered. "And until the big guys are locked up, I'm still in danger."

"Hey," he said, and gently clasped her upper arms. "I won't let anything happen to you."

"I'm scared, Ethan." Finally saying it aloud sent another wave of shivers down her body.

"It's okay, honey." He drew her close and she didn't resist.

Despite knowing it wasn't a good idea, she laid her head on his solid chest, listening to the even thumps of his heart. He softly stroked her back, and she snuggled closer, remembering their first kiss. The way he'd been so sweet, asking if he could kiss her before taking like the only other boy who'd kissed her before then. Ethan's gentleness and consideration had won her heart that day, and right now, she wasn't so sure he didn't still have a big piece of it.

She leaned back and looked up at him. Got lost in his eyes. He let her go and reached up to cup her face, then slid his fingers into her hair. He was going to kiss her. She couldn't breathe. Couldn't look away. Couldn't do anything but wait for his lips to descend on hers.

Her phone chimed from her pocket, sounding like a warning alarm. She jerked back and dug it out, keeping her gaze from Ethan. No sense in letting him see the effect he still had on her.

She looked at the screen and worked hard to catch a full breath. "It's Stacey from the newspaper," she said, thinking about what would have happened without this interruption and surprised by how much she wished Stacey hadn't called.

Ethan sighed out a deep breath. "Don't answer. They could be tracking your calls."

"This could be about the shoot. I need to talk to her."

He dug out his cell. "Use my phone to call her back."

Jennie took it, careful not to touch him and reignite the firestorm that just passed between them. She dialed the office and then hit thirty-three for Stacey's extension.

"Hey, Stacey. It's Jennie. Did you just call?" She forced her tone to be relaxed, though her heart was still thumping wildly.

"Thank goodness I got a hold of you. Two detectives from the police department are here. They want you to come in and talk to them about the break-in at that gallery."

"Now?"

"They said it's urgent."

"Hold on." She put her hand over the phone and turned to Ethan, finally looking up at him and nearly wilting under his heated gaze. "Two detectives are at my office and they want to talk to me."

"Someone could be watching for you there." He clipped his words as if the thought upset him. "See if you can meet them somewhere else."

"Where?"

He paused. "On second thought, it'd probably be

best for us to go there. If Sotos's thugs are watching the detectives, they'll lead them to you no matter the location we set up. Plus we know the logistics of your office better than any other neutral location."

"So yes, then?"

"Maybe. Put Stacey on speaker so we both can talk to her."

"She'll ask who you are."

"Tell her the truth."

"Sorry to keep you waiting, Stacey. I've been working with a private investigations agency since the break-in, and one of the investigators wants to talk to you before I meet with the detective. I'm putting you on speaker. Okay?"

"Sure," Stacey answered, seemingly intrigued.

"Hi, Stacey," Ethan said. "Have you asked to see the detectives' identification?"

"No."

"Could you do so and give me their names, please?"

"Sure. Hold on."

"Sounds like you think these guys aren't legit." Unease settling in, Jennie looked up at him to gauge his mood.

"I'm just being cautious. Once I have their names, I'll have Kat check them out. I want to be sure they're the detectives who caught the case before I let you meet with them."

"Their names are Victor Tilden and Nathan Winters," Stacey said.

"And their IDs look legit?" Ethan asked.

Stacey laughed. "I guess so. They look official, anyway."

"Okay. Tell them the meet's a go. If something changes, we'll get back to you."

"Bye, Stacey, and thanks," Jennie added.

"You might as well go back to work." Ethan took his phone from her. "It'll take a while to check them out and make arrangements for safe transport if they're legit."

She nodded and closed the door between them. She went to the enlarger and tried to focus on the paper, but she couldn't concentrate. The fear he'd so readily helped her put at bay while he held her a few moments ago returned tenfold.

She wrapped her arms around her stomach as if she could comfort herself as well as Ethan had. But it did no good. The fear settled in deeper and she hoped— no, prayed—that if they did leave the safety of this place to meet with the detectives that the good Lord above didn't want her to die today.

Ethan sat behind the wheel of his truck with Jennie peering anxiously out the window. Once they reached the newspaper office, they'd form a transfer detail much like yesterday minus Kat. Derrick and Cole both needed a break from Madeline's high-strung ways, and Kat eagerly volunteered to take on Madeline, a true sign of how desperate his sister was to get out of the office.

With the way he'd just acted in the darkroom, he should let Kat handle Jennie's protection. He'd thought he merely wanted to comfort her, but within a few seconds, he'd known it was more. Even after her phone rang and he needed to focus on the details of the case, he still wanted to kiss her. Something he couldn't do. He drew in a deep breath and sighed out his stress.

"What's wrong?" she asked him.

"Nothing, why?" He tried for a lighthearted tone, but could tell by her expression that he failed.

Her gaze intensified. "I remember that sigh. You only sighed like that when a problem was brewing."

"No problem." Not unless he acted on his feelings again.

"Did you learn something about the cartel that you're not telling me?"

"No."

"So what is it, then?" She cast a look of frustration at him, reminding him so much of their past together.

He laughed, enjoying the feel of lightening up. "I'd forgotten how you never let things go."

"I let things go all the time."

He eyed her up. "Not with me, you didn't."

"I've changed since then, Ethan. You must not have noticed."

"Believe me. I've noticed everything."

He studied her, and her face turned a crimson-red. "Mind telling me why it's bothering you so much?"

She sighed and looked at her hands. "I don't think

it's a good idea to do anything that might lead us down a path we have no business going down."

"And what path would that be?"

"Me and you. Us. Another relationship. Call it whatever you want, but it's not a good idea."

"What makes you think I'm even thinking about it?"

Her head popped up. "Aren't you?"

"Even if I am, would it do any good? Has anything changed between us?"

She didn't respond but leaned her chin on her fist, looking out the window. A sure sign she didn't plan to say anything more.

Except for the aversion she had to talking about the past, she'd always been direct and outspoken. That was one of her traits that he found so appealing. But she'd used that directness against him when she'd ended their relationship, and she was using it against him now, trying to keep him at arm's length.

He felt a heaviness in his heart. Not for her or all the struggles she'd faced, but selfishly, for himself. It was now perfectly clear that he still cared about her. He didn't want to have feelings for her, but she still had all of the same traits he'd once fallen in love with, and he could easily see himself falling hopelessly in love with her again. The ending would be slightly different, but he would end it, of that he was certain. He'd be a fool if he let things get out of hand between them and give her a chance to walk out on him again.

TEN

A tense silence filled the truck until they arrived at her office, and Jennie was thankful for it. Well, maybe not thankful that it was tense, but she was glad Ethan had clammed up and not spoken another word for the rest of the drive. Maybe he'd finally realized that she didn't fit in his life and she'd done the right thing in leaving him.

That was what she wanted, right? So why did it feel as if someone had filled her heart with lead?

"Did you hear me, Jen?" He peered at her across the seat, concern marring his handsome face.

"I got it. Stay between you and Cole and don't dawdle."

"Okay, then, let's go." He slid out and ran around the front, looking right then left as he moved.

Cole stood outside her door and when Ethan joined him, he opened it.

"All clear inside," Cole reported, and Ethan gave a nod of understanding.

Jennie shouldered her gadget bag and tote containing the negatives. Neither she nor Ethan wanted to leave the negatives and CD at the darkroom. These, coupled with the bulky vest, made her feel as graceful as an elephant as she slid out.

Ethan cupped her elbow, urging her forward. Derrick, who looked like a copy of Dani, only taller and all male, waited a few feet ahead. As she started forward, they made a circle of protection around her until she entered the building.

"Afternoon, Ms. Buchanan." Max, the security guard, watched her detail with a raised brow.

"Hi, Max," she answered with a light tone, hoping to defuse his interest in her entourage. But it didn't work. Max gaped at them until she and Ethan boarded the elevator. Ethan's siblings stayed in the lobby. As the doors closed, Ethan directed a warning look at Cole, who acknowledged it with a clipped nod.

This was all too surreal for her normally boring life. She didn't wear a bulky vest out in public, and big, hunky men with guns didn't usually surround her and escort her into the office.

She couldn't help but laugh.

"What's so funny?" Ethan asked and seemed to relax a notch.

"I feel like I'm in an action movie with Bruce Willis or something."

Instead of getting mad at her teasing as she thought he might do, he chuckled. "So which one of us is Bruce?"

"You, of course." She wrinkled her nose at him.

He turned a thousand-watt smile on her, and it shot

through every nerve ending in her body, making her very aware of the strong man who was oh, so wrong for her.

When the doors slid open again, he replaced his smile with an intense look that did a far different number on her nerves. Power emanated from him, and at that moment, she knew beyond any doubt that he would do anything to protect her.

It was a heady feeling to think that a man this powerful and commanding would give up even his life for her. So when he quirked a finger at her from outside the elevator, it took her a minute before stepping out of the elevator and heading toward her cubicle.

"Slow down." He came up beside her, his breath whispering over her neck and sending her heart thumping again. "Let me check things out first."

They went into her work area, and she spotted the two officers waiting to talk with her. One of them was tall and thin, and reminded her of a string bean. The other was short with wide shoulders, a thick neck and massive thighs. Both had blond hair and wore dark-colored suits. String Bean's hung limply but Muscles' seemed to strain at his mass.

"Stay behind me," Ethan warned and slowly moved toward the detectives. At a wide column, he pivoted. "Stay behind this pillar until I tell you to join us. Got it?"

"Got it," she answered quietly, hoping to soften his gaze and succeeding.

He gave her arm a quick squeeze before going to the detectives. "Identification, please."

She peeked around the column and saw String Bean fix a harsh stare on Ethan. "And who are you?"

"Not important. If you want to talk with Ms. Buchanan, you'll show me your ID."

String Bean reached inside his suit jacket, and as he did, Ethan's hand went for his gun. The short officer did the same thing.

"You got a permit for that?" String Bean raised a brow.

"We'll talk about that after I see your ID."

Both detectives flashed a badge.

"Not so fast." Ethan eyed up String Bean. "I'd like a closer look."

String Bean looked mad, but he complied, holding out his badge for closer inspection. Ethan studied it then lifted his hand and beckoned her with a curl of his finger.

"About that permit," String Bean said.

Ethan withdrew his wallet and showed the detective a card that looked similar to a driver's license.

String Bean gave a nod then turned to her. "You must be Ms. Buchanan."

"I am."

"Is there someplace more private where we can talk?" He issued a friendly smile then looked around.

Jennie followed his gaze and saw the office staff peering over their cubicles.

"My workstation is private." She started forward, and Ethan stepped in front of her.

He checked out her space then motioned for her to enter. His phone rang and he glanced at caller ID before answering. "You have news for me, Jack?"

After all their setbacks and roadblocks, this call from Ethan's FBI buddy had to be good news. Maybe they'd succeeded in enhancing the photos and identifying the men so the officers sliding past Ethan would finally be able to make an arrest and her life could go back to normal.

The detectives took a seat in chairs facing her desk, and Muscles draped his jacket on the back of his chair. She set her bags on her desk and ripped off her bulky vest while waiting to see what Ethan was going to do.

"Jack," he said. "Are you there?" He stared at his phone, a puzzled look on his face.

"Reception is awful in here," she offered and pointed at the other end of the open space. "It's better over by the windows."

His gaze followed the direction of her finger then he looked back at her as if he didn't want to leave.

"Go," she said. "I'll be fine with the detectives."

He glanced at her one more time before taking off. She focused on the two men in her cubicle. They hadn't introduced themselves. Not that she really cared. Ethan had gotten their particulars, and even if they did tell her their names, she'd still think of them as String Bean and Muscles.

String Bean slid forward and rested a pointy elbow

on her desk. "I suppose you know we're here about the gallery break-in and vandalism."

She nodded and waited for more specifics before saying anything.

"As you also know, the photos were too damaged to determine why the intruder took such extreme measures to destroy them." Muscles shifted on his chair as if he couldn't get comfortable. "So we hoped you'd be able to provide us with copies of the photos for our review."

She wasn't about to give them the pictures she'd already printed as she'd need them for the showing. "Unfortunately I don't have any hard copies to spare."

"But you're working on printing more pictures, right?"

Their question caught her by surprise for a moment, but thanks to Linda, this was public knowledge. Since they were investigating this case, they probably knew a whole lot more. "I can't give those to you if I'm to make opening night at the gallery."

"Are you working from digital files or negatives?" String Bean asked.

"Negatives, but I have digital files, as well."

"We'd like a copy of the digital files, then." String Bean's tone said, *Don't mess with me, honey. Just hand over the files.*

Should she tell them that they'd been through many of the photos and the FBI was already working on one of them? If she did, Ethan's friend at the FBI could get in trouble for interfering with the investigation.

Besides, she didn't even know if the picture could be improved enough to yield any results. And what harm would it do to have the police working on the images, too?

"I'll make copies for you." She reached for her gadget bag and pulled out the CD.

While she waited for the files to complete copying, she checked her email. She was vaguely aware of the detectives signaling to each other in some code they'd probably developed over the years, but her inbox held hundreds of messages and demanded her full attention. She scrolled down the names and opened a message from her boss. She confirmed that she would meet the reporter at the shoot tomorrow. In all the turmoil, she'd almost forgotten about tomorrow's shoot.

Her computer dinged, and she ejected the copied CD before putting the original back in her bag.

"Is this all you need?" She stood and handed the CD to String Bean, following it with a smile in hopes of ending this conversation so she could get back to work.

He returned the smile. "Actually, we recovered something else at the gallery that we need you to take a look at."

"Okay," she answered and waited for them to show it to her.

"It's in our car," Muscles explained. "We couldn't bring it up here, so we'll need you to come with us."

"I don't know if I should leave right now." She cast a glance in Ethan's direction, but she couldn't see over the top of the cubicles.

"It'll take just a minute." Muscles rose and took his jacket from the back of the chair. "We're parked in the loading dock so you'll be safe. Plus, we'll escort you both ways." He didn't wait for her agreement but gripped her elbow, directing her out of the cubicle.

She suddenly felt uncomfortable and tried to back away. Something hard poked into her side. She looked down.

A gun? He had a gun?

Her heart sank then started thumping wildly. "What's going on?"

He draped his jacket over the weapon. "We're gonna go for a little ride. If you make even a peep, I'll use this on your coworkers. You got that, little lady?"

"But what—"

"Just do as we say and everyone will be fine." He jabbed the gun harder. "Now smile at the woman across the aisle."

String Bean grabbed both of her bags and waited for them to exit.

Jennie tried to catch Belinda's attention, but she kept her head down and her fingers flew over her keyboard. Jennie knew Belinda saw them. She never missed anything.

Jennie tried clearing her throat to get her attention.

"One more false move and someone gets it," Muscles whispered from behind, his foul breath making her stomach churn. "Nod if you understand."

She nodded and made her way slowly to the end of

the cubicles, searching for any form of rescue. At the end of the aisle, she peered in Ethan's direction, but a deliveryman pushing a large copier down the aisle blocked any visual of him. Muscles urged her toward the freight elevator where String Bean punched the down button.

The whir of cables moved the car toward them and toward her certain death if she didn't get free. Once they got her in the elevator, she was a goner. The urge to run nearly overpowered her. But she couldn't endanger her friends.

The door opened and Muscles shoved her into the car. He removed his jacket from the gun and held it out, his eyes daring her to make a break for it. She stood, mute and silent.

String Bean slithered in and stood at her side. "We make pretty good cops, huh? Even your hotshot bodyguard believed it."

As the doors closed, fear finally got the best of her and she started trembling. What did these thugs plan to do to her?

"Where are you taking me?" she asked, her voice coming out just above a whisper.

"The boss wants to have a word with you."

She drew in a breath. Pulled deep, but her lungs refused to expand.

She tried harder, coming up short and feeling faint.

She imagined herself standing before Sotos, who declared she must die. Movies she'd seen with drug lords torturing then killing people who crossed them ran through her mind.

Gory. Bloody. Harsh. They died in great pain and anguish.

"Breathe, lady," Muscles said, his tone grating and nasty. "This might be the last chance you'll get."

ELEVEN

"And you're sure it's Eduardo Sotos in the picture?" Ethan asked one more time, hoping he hadn't heard Jack clearly. Sure, he'd known the Sotos gang was involved, but he'd still hoped that the instigator was someone lower down in the organization—not Sotos himself.

"That's what I said for about the eightieth time," Jack replied in a sarcastic tone.

"Look. I'm sorry, but this case is going nowhere fast. Even if we do finally figure out why Sotos doesn't want this picture to get out, unless it's evidence enough to arrest him on its own, he won't stop until he has everything he wants."

"Sounds like you're gonna need the DEA's help."

"You have any contacts there?" Ethan asked.

"Maybe. But it's a long shot."

"Mind making a call about this and showing them the picture? They may recognize the guy with Sotos."

"You got it. I'll let you know if I find anything out."

They disconnected and Ethan shoved his phone into his pocket as he headed back to Jennie's cubicle. He hated to tell her about Sotos, but he needed to be honest with her regardless of the fear it would cause. He slowed and eased toward her cubicle, hoping to catch the thread of their conversation before he arrived so he'd be prepared.

Silence.

He paused and waited for someone to speak.

More silence.

He glanced around the cubicle wall. The visitors' chairs were empty, and Jennie's vest hung on the corner of her chair.

Panic rose up.

Calm down, Ethan. She's with cops. She's fine.

Wrong. She wasn't fine until he made sure of it.

He spun toward the cubicle across the aisle.

"Did you see where Jennie went?" he asked the woman looking up at him.

"Uh…I…I don't know."

"This could be a life-and-death matter. If you saw or heard anything, I need to know." He infused his words with urgency yet tried to keep down the mounting panic.

"The cops said they had something in their car that she needed to see, and she went with them to the elevator."

"How long ago?"

"Not long. Maybe five minutes."

"Thanks." Ethan took off.

"Not that way," the woman called after him. "The freight elevator to the loading dock."

"Where?" he asked.

She pointed in the other direction.

He reversed course. He'd never been so thankful for an office busybody. At the elevator, he punched the down button. No response from the elevator.

No time to wait. Only three floors in the building—he'd take the stairs. He flew down them, lifting his cell as he went. Cole answered on the third ring, but the call broke up and he couldn't understand his brother.

He kept Cole on the line and pushed through the door. A narrow hallway led to another heavy fire door. He was through it in seconds and let his gaze slide over the cavernous space. An unmarked black sedan idled in the main receiving area. The burly detective held his gun on Jennie, and it looked as if he was forcing her into the car.

Ethan drew his gun and started toward them.

"Ethan," he heard Cole say from the phone still in his hand.

"Bring the car to the loading dock," he answered. "They have Jennie."

The tall guy spotted him, drew his weapon then shoved it in Jennie's temple. "Come any closer and she's dead."

Fear, raw and primal, darkened Jennie's eyes and bit into Ethan's heart. He'd failed her. Now they had her, and he couldn't stop them without risking her life.

"Get in the car or I'll plug your bodyguard," the shorter man said to Jennie, his gun out now and aimed at Ethan.

She gave Ethan an apologetic look then climbed into the car.

What was she apologizing for? For going with them? Why wouldn't she trust detectives? They'd even fooled Ethan. Kat had cleared the names and he'd swear their IDs were legitimate. Still, he shouldn't have left her with them. But he needed to quit blaming himself. He'd have plenty of time to do that once they got her back. He had to get her back.

The short guy got behind the wheel and the tall guy jumped in next to Jennie. They screeched onto the street. Horns blared and brakes squealed.

Ethan bolted after them but hung back so they couldn't see him. He watched the car until it moved out of view then he charged down the sidewalk to keep them in sight. Cole careened the SUV up to the corner, and Ethan scrambled into the back.

"Black sedan. Two blocks up. Two armed men have Jennie. Get a move on but be discreet."

Cole floored it as if he hadn't heard Ethan.

"C'mon, man," Ethan said. "If they make us this is all over."

"I know what I'm doing, bro," Cole said. "What happened?"

Ethan told him. "No need to ream me for my carelessness."

"Hey," Cole said and eased up on the gas. "Any one of us might've done the same thing."

Might've was the key word in that response.

"So you think these are dirty cops or imposters?" Derrick asked.

"I don't know. Their IDs were top-notch if they were fakes."

"Want me to check on them?" As a former Portland homicide detective, Derrick could easily find out what they were dealing with here.

"Yeah." Ethan gave Derrick the detectives' last names, and his youngest brother phoned the Portland Police Bureau.

Ethan tuned out Derrick's conversation. He didn't really want to know the answer. If the badges were fakes, he'd been duped in the worst way. It'd be hard to forgive himself for such a stupid mistake. Better to concentrate on the road.

Cole was winding in and out of traffic and tailing the sedan at a good distance. Ethan wanted to jump up front and drive, but that would only slow them down. Not that Cole would even turn over the steering wheel. Just a year younger than Ethan, Cole more than any of the other siblings pushed Ethan's perceived authority based on age. There'd always been a hint of competition between them. Nothing major, just a sliver of disquiet.

Cole had come to the family when Ethan was seven, ending his status as the only child. Ethan had wanted a brother. He just wasn't prepared to share his parents with another kid. Little did he know at the time that there would be three more children to come. But in the end, they'd all formed a tight bond and he'd rather be with his siblings in this race to save Jennie than anyone else.

"There," he called out. "They're headed onto the 405." Ethan watched them climb the ramp to the highway.

"Relax. I see them," Cole said.

When they made the same turn, Ethan sought out the other car. He spotted them merging into traffic and let out a breath. They were heading east and if they kept on this route, they would merge onto I-5, which they did, flying over the Marquam Bridge and heading north.

"The real detectives are in the office right now," Derrick said and stowed his phone.

"So maybe we should back off and get them to pursue," Cole suggested.

"No police," Ethan answered.

Derrick turned and eyed him up. "Are you sure about that?"

"Look, little brother. I know you were once one of them and think they can do no wrong, but if we call this in, what do you think they'll do?"

"Put top priority on it and send out a show of force."

"And what will happen then?" Ethan let his words sit for a moment. "They'll force these creeps into shooting Jennie. We can't risk it."

"You act like the officers don't know how to handle this."

"You know as well as I do some of them don't. All

it takes is one rookie doing the wrong thing and Jennie dies."

Derrick rolled his eyes. "We'll do this your way, but if we lose the car, we're calling it in."

Cole scoffed. "Like I'm gonna lose them."

"We need to quit talking and keep our eyes on the vehicle so that doesn't happen." Ethan sat forward, craning his neck to be sure the car remained in view. Finally, they exited on Marine Drive and into the industrial district lining the Willamette River.

"Looks like they're taking her to a warehouse." Derrick stated the obvious.

"Not good," Cole added as if they needed to hear it.

Ethan held his tongue and watched three additional men armed with assault weapons acknowledge the car's arrival. The sedan pulled up to the warehouse door and parked, while the gunmen disappeared via a side entry.

Ethan fought down a wave of fear. "With that kind of firepower, if they get her inside, we'll never get her back."

"What do you suggest?" Cole slowed and parked out of view.

"Jennie's in the back," Derrick jumped in. "So I'd ram them in the front, pushing them up against the building. The driver won't be able to get out and we can retrieve Jennie before both men recover from the shock."

"It'll also block the door and keep the men inside," Cole said.

"What if there's a back door?" Ethan respected his brothers' tactical skills, but it wasn't that simple. "Plus we could damage our engine and not be able to drive off. The air bags would deploy, too, temporarily blocking your line of sight."

"We could back into them," Cole suggested.

"And we can be out and on these two creeps before they recover," Derrick added. "If there is a back door we'd still be able to rescue her before anyone can get around the building."

"I don't know," Ethan said, second-guessing himself. "Maybe I was wrong before. Maybe we should call in backup and wait."

"Then we'll have a hostage situation and these guys have nothing to lose," Derrick said.

"Fine, we'll do it. But be sure to stay well away from Jennie," Ethan directed. "Derrick, you're first in. Get a bead on the driver and hold him at bay. I'll cover the man in back and get Jennie out. Cole, you're backup. Make sure the vehicle is ready to retreat."

"Oh, yeah." Cole grinned.

Ethan couldn't grin, but he liked seeing the rare smile on his brother's face. "If everything goes okay, we should try to take these men into custody, as well. But one sign of their pals from inside and we're out of here. Got it?"

Derrick nodded and Cole reversed into place then floored it.

Ethan watched out the rear and braced for the

impact. He saw surprise flash on Jennie's face and watched her scoot to the far side of the car.

Lord, please don't let her be harmed in this maneuver.

The car crashed. Metal screamed. They jostled back and forth. Derrick pushed his door open only seconds before Ethan. Guns drawn, they jumped out. Derrick charged at the front door and Ethan the back.

Derrick aimed his gun at the driver through the window. Ethan jerked open the back door, caught a quick view of Jennie moving. Good, she was alive.

He directed his gun at the passenger and glared at him. "Weapons in the air. Both of you. Try anything and you're dead."

He wanted to search Jennie for injuries, but that would have to come later. He kept his gaze locked with the man in the backseat and waited as both men held up their guns. He took them one at a time and tucked them into his belt.

He reached for Jennie's hand. "C'mon, Jen. You're coming with me."

She grabbed her bags then clasped his hand, and the warmth shot all the way to his heart, flooding him with relief. Relief that he had to ignore right now. He needed to keep his wits about him and get her to safety. Then he could revel in finding her safe.

"You got 'em," he told Derrick, who nodded his response.

Ethan put Jennie behind him and backed toward the SUV. They moved past Cole now standing on the running board and aiming at the sedan. Ethan helped Jennie into the back and slid in behind her.

"Get down," he instructed her and gently pushed her to the floor. "We're good to go."

"Two automatics at your nine o'clock," Cole called out to Derrick. "Get out of there now!"

Derrick backed toward the car, climbed in and leaned out his open window with his gun trained on the men so Cole could slide behind the wheel.

"Go. Go. Go." Derrick's excitement matched the adrenaline flowing through Ethan.

Cole floored the gas and the tires spun then gripped. Derrick slid in and closed the window. Gravel and dust peppered the air. Gunshots pelted the car. Ethan held his breath as they raced off and the fire of weapons died down.

"Call this in, Derrick," Ethan said, his voice alive with adrenaline as he turned his attention to Jennie. He lifted her to the seat and scanned her from head to toe. A nasty bruise had already formed on her cheek, marring the creamy complexion. She was shaking, and as her eyes met his, fat tears slipped down her cheeks.

"Hey," he said, feeling like a first-class loser for letting this happen to her. He cupped her cheek. "Don't cry."

"Thank you," she managed to say between chattering teeth.

"For what, Jen? Letting these guys get to you?"

"No. It was my fault. I should have found a way to get away from them before this happened."

"I shouldn't have let you out of my sight."

"Hey," Derrick called over the seat, "how about you both stop with the blame and celebrate the fact that everything turned out fine?"

Ethan peered at her. "You are okay, aren't you?" He gently rubbed his thumb over the bruise. "This happen when we hit the car?"

"No. When they shoved me inside."

He stifled a curse and drew her into his arms, holding her as tight as he dared without bruising her more. He wanted to kiss her. Right here in the car in front of his brothers.

But he couldn't, could he? She didn't want him to. Those creeps might've tried to do her harm, but nothing else had changed.

Jennie let Ethan hold her. Not only let him, wanted him to. She'd been so afraid. Terrified, actually. Now she was safe. God had sent Ethan and his brothers to her rescue.

Thank You, Father. For not only keeping me safe, but for the Justice siblings. For their safety. And I pray You continue to watch over all of us, keep us from all harm and let us find the men behind this before someone else is injured.

She pushed back a few inches and looked at Ethan. The pain etched in his startling black eyes sent her heart into a spin.

He cared about her. She'd been prickly since they'd reconnected and still he cared. He was the only man, person actually, who'd ever cared this much for her, and she was in awe of his depth of compassion.

How could she ever have left him for any reason?

He eased back more. "Are you sure you're all right?"

"Yes," she whispered.

"The crash didn't hurt you?"

"No. I saw you coming."

"Promise me something." His eyes were fixed on hers.

"Anything."

"If I let you out of my or my family's sight again before this is resolved, stop me. Okay?"

The softness of his voice brought more tears to her eyes and they rolled down her cheeks.

"And don't cry." His voice was low and intimate. "I can't handle it when you cry."

Despite the two men in the front seat, she felt as if she and Ethan were alone. She reached a hand toward him, but he groaned, and with his eyes still fixed on hers, he set her away.

She caught Cole's glance in the mirror and suddenly felt self-conscious. What was she thinking, fawning over Ethan like that in front of his brothers? Fawning over him in *any* situation was wrong.

"Where to, bro?" Cole asked.

"Kat's house to regroup. And let's be sure no one's tailing us."

Cole gave a clipped nod, and Jennie saw him check the mirrors.

The adrenaline started leaving her body, and she

felt weak with relief. She was with Ethan. Safe again. But for how long?

She faced him. "Did Jack have any news?"

He didn't answer right away, and she knew that meant bad news. She braced herself to hear it.

"One of the men in the picture is Eduardo Sotos."

"And the other guy?"

"No ID, but Jack's calling the DEA to see if we can get a lead on him."

Everything they had feared was true. She'd caught a ruthless killer in one of her pictures. So now what would happen?

She lay back on the seat and closed her eyes. Her cheek throbbed, bringing Ethan's gentle touch to mind. Why was she always falling for the wrong guy?

First as a teen, mistakenly believing the boy who fathered her baby wanted more than a casual fling. Then as an adult, she'd only had three serious relationships, but none of them should ever have happened. She should've called things off with Ethan the moment she realized the difference in their backgrounds. Wes was a mistake from day one. He was just her rebound guy. And most recently, Owen, well, she should've told him about the baby right up front, and they'd never have gone on more than a few dates.

But none of that mattered. Not now. Not when a drug lord was after her.

She felt the car slow and turn a few corners then climb up a steep hill. It slowed even more and they

Double Exposure

bumped into the driveway before coming to a complete stop. She sat up and waited for directions.

"Check things out, Derrick." Ethan's tone still held worry. "We'll wait here until you clear the house."

"I'll go with him to speed things up," Cole offered and climbed out with his younger brother.

"You still doing okay?" Ethan asked.

"As good as I can be after what happened."

"I know I promised never to bring this up again, but in light of what just happened, I wondered if you'd consider canceling the show."

She had thought about that the entire time the two creeps held her at gunpoint in their car. She'd said to herself, *If I get out of this alive, I'll back off.* Now she wasn't sure what to do.

"Jen," Ethan said gently.

"I want to cancel it—even thought about it when they had me—but now…"

"Now that you're safe you can't," he finished for her.

"I'm sorry, Ethan."

"I understand up here." He paused and tapped his temple. "But I don't fully understand what motivates you."

"You can't. Not unless you've walked in my shoes." She sighed and looked out the window. "Every time I think about these kids, I ache with the hunger of my childhood. Empty cupboards and my stomach growling, keeping me awake all night. Going to school the next day and hiding in the bathroom at lunchtime so I wouldn't have to see other kids eat and then toss good food into the trash when they were full. Eating plain rice meal after meal because it was cheap."

"Did your father ever apply for assistance?"

"He was too proud. Said he'd provide or we wouldn't eat." She felt the weight of her childhood bearing down on her. "And it wasn't just the food, Ethan. The smell of poverty still clings to me. Apartments that reeked from neglect. I cleaned and bathed as often as possible but it never left me." She looked at the ceiling to hold back her tears. "I told you I joined the yearbook staff to go to events, but I really did it to get away from the places where we lived and the creepy men who lived nearby."

"I'm sorry, honey," Ethan said so softly that she looked back at him and let his warm expression comfort her before going on.

"I wanted to get away from it so badly. I thought about leaving during college but I only made enough money to pay for things my scholarships didn't cover. I kept telling myself a few more years in that dump would help me live a lifetime free of poverty." She shuddered.

"It tears me up inside to think of you living that way." Ethan drew her into his arms again and she willingly let him. "Especially when I knew you and could have done something about it. I wish you'd told me."

"I didn't want your pity," she whispered into the curve of his neck. She settled closer, reveling in his clean scent that drove out all the horrible odors of her past.

The door opened, and she jerked back.

"We're clear," Cole said, giving them both an appraising look. "You can go in now."

Jennie didn't wait to be told again but bolted from the car, into the house and up the stairs to the guest room. She'd told Ethan things she'd never shared with anyone—things she'd never wanted him to know.

All those years of hiding her upbringing from others. Being like her father. Too prideful to accept help or let others know what was going on. She'd thought finally talking about her childhood might free her from the shame she carried, but embarrassment still sat in a lump in her stomach. She didn't think she could look at Ethan again. Not without seeing pity coloring the eyes that had once looked on her with total and complete love.

TWELVE

Derrick left for his shift on Madeline's detail, and Ethan watched Jennie run up the stairs. He'd always wanted her to share her past with him, and now that she had, he didn't know what to do. She was right. He did feel badly for her. How could he not? No child deserved a life like that. But it was precisely that life that had given her the passion to help others and made her the special person she was today.

Cole came up beside him. "I guess this thing with Jennie isn't over."

Ethan looked at his brother and wanted to tell him to mind his own business, but maybe if they discussed this, Cole could help him work though the problem.

"Can we talk for a minute?" Ethan asked.

Cole was clearly surprised but he nodded.

"Let's get something to drink." Ethan went to the kitchen. He handed Cole his usual cola and took a bottle of water for himself.

He climbed onto a stool at the counter. "You ever want something that's really bad for you?"

Cole raised a discerning eyebrow. "You mean recently?"

"I'm not talking about kid stuff here." Ethan knew his tone was defensive.

"You're talking about Jennie."

"Yeah."

"From all I can see, the two of you are adults, not involved with someone else, so why is she so wrong?"

"I've had enough of women saying they want a relationship then bailing when things get serious."

"You're talking about Carla."

"Jennie and Carla both took off. Maybe Jennie's like Carla and I'm just attracted to the kind of woman who can't commit."

"She is nothing like Carla." He shot Ethan an impatient look.

Ethan studied his brother, who rarely weighed in on issues lately. To do so meant he had strong opinions on Carla.

"Don't look so shocked," Cole said. "I never thought Carla was the right person for you."

"And yet you never told me."

"Would you have listened if I had?"

Would he? Or would he have done just what he wanted, ignoring help from the brother who'd lived hard and lost hard? Whose take on life might be jaded? Whose fiancée bailed on him for no good reason other than she didn't want to marry a man in law enforcement? Who had to live through unspeakable tragedies when his National Guard platoon had been called up?

Who—now that Ethan thought about it—had come to be a great judge of people because he'd said farewell to all the social pleasantries of life and saw people for what they were?

Still, Ethan wouldn't have listened. "No. Probably not."

"But you're willing to listen to me now?"

"I guess…I mean…I don't know."

"I think you're missing the most obvious thing here. Jennie's already proven to all of us that she can commit. Sotos's thugs kidnap her and she still won't cancel the show. Doesn't that say she isn't afraid of commitment?"

"I don't know, man."

Cole clapped Ethan on the back. "For such a smart guy, you're pretty dense at times."

That didn't deserve a response so Ethan stared at his brother and waited for him to explain.

"Change the way you think," Cole said, "and there's no problem."

"It's not that easy, bro."

"Why not?"

"What if we're wrong? What if I put myself out there and she bails again?"

"Then she bails and you pick up the pieces."

"You of all people know that's not as easy as it sounds."

"Honestly." Cole stood. "It's just that easy. We aren't talking about people dying in a war or children losing mothers and fathers in combat. Or even innocent civilians being cut down. We're talking about your feelings. If you want to be alone for the rest of your life, run the other way. If not, deal and tell her how you feel."

The sound of the front door opening cut through the space and both of them turned to wait for whoever arrived.

"Hello," Kat called. "Where is everyone?"

"In here," Cole answered then took a long drink of his soda.

Kat came into the room. "Where's Jennie?"

"Upstairs," Ethan said.

"Wow! That was some crazy kind of scary, huh? Is she all right?"

"She'll be fine," Ethan said, but he wasn't sure either of them would ever be fine again.

Jennie didn't want to eat anything, but she couldn't let food go to waste, so she choked down the lasagna Kat made for dinner. Jennie was sure it was good, but it tasted like sawdust to her. Her revelation to Ethan about her squalid past and residual fear over the cartel kept her stomach knotted, and the conversation flowing around the table didn't help.

Cole and Ethan sat at the heads of the table, and Kat across from her. Kat kept giving Jennie concerned looks, and Ethan avoided looking at her at all. Just as she'd suspected he'd do. He didn't know what to say to her after the emotional bomb she had dropped in the car.

Still, she couldn't seem to quit looking at him and

remembering the rescue. He hadn't batted an eyelash or shown any fear, but saved her from two armed thugs. True, he'd had his brothers' help, but he'd led the charge, and she respected him even more than before. He stood strong and true. Dependable. A force she'd hate to come up against.

"Did you hear me, Jennie?" Kat asked.

"Huh?" Jennie looked at Kat.

"I was wondering if you wanted to help me get dessert."

"Sure," Jennie answered cheerfully, even though Kat's look declared she had something on her mind and she planned to share it once out of the room.

Jennie followed Kat into the kitchen, where she'd already uncovered a pan of brownies and pulled out a knife. "You cut and I'll serve."

"Do you have a plastic knife?" Jennie asked.

"Sure. Why?"

"Brownies don't stick to plastic like they do real silverware."

Kat raised a perfectly groomed brow. "I never took you for the domestic type."

"Oh, really, what type am I?" Jennie's tone was harsh, probably from the feeling of inferiority that clung to her from her discussion this afternoon.

"Relax, Jennie. I'm not judging you."

Jennie simply lifted her brow and waited for Kat to continue.

"You travel all the time, so I figured you don't spend a lot of time in the kitchen."

Kat's statement hurt for some reason, and Jennie couldn't pinpoint why. "I don't cook much."

"See, I wasn't wrong." Kat dug a plastic knife out of the drawer and handed it to Jennie. "Watching you over the past few days, I've gotten the sense that you're driven by something that won't let you settle down and keeps you so focused. This whole thing with the Sotos gang hasn't stopped you. I admire your determination."

"Thanks, Kat." Jennie sliced the brownies.

Kat scooped them out and plated them. "There's just one thing."

Jennie knew that compliment was going to be followed by something else. She'd just felt it. She looked up. "What?"

"I see the way you're looking at Ethan, and I don't like it."

"Excuse me?"

"I don't like it, Jennie. Not that I don't like you. I do. But it took Ethan years to get over you the first time. If he falls for you again—" Kat paused and stared at Jennie "—and I want to go on record as saying he seems to be heading that way—I don't think he'll recover a second time when you leave him."

Jennie hated that Kat had predicted a future Jennie thought was all too likely, but she wouldn't admit it. "What makes you so sure I'd leave?"

Kat's gaze softened. "I'm pretty sure you haven't reconciled the issue that sent you running the first time."

"And how do you know that?"

"Because your eyes are still haunted." Kat's gaze lingered for a few moments then she went back to plating brownies.

Jennie didn't know how to respond. Kat was a keen observer if she could see what Jennie had years of practice hiding. Or maybe her time with Ethan had simply brought it closer to the surface.

"Don't hurt my brother, Jennie, or you'll deal with me." Kat fixed a stare on Jennie that she must have used as a police officer. "We understand each other?"

"Yes," Jennie answered.

Kat took the brownies and a stack of plates then headed back into the other room.

Jennie couldn't follow. Not until she composed herself.

Kat was right. Jennie hadn't resolved any of her feelings, and if she was dumb enough to succumb to the emotions for Ethan tumbling through her heart and lead him on, she deserved every bit of Kat's wrath.

Ethan didn't know what had gone on in the kitchen, but when Jennie returned to the dining room, she slipped quietly into her chair, looking as if his sister had beaten her up. Not physically, although the bruise on her cheek was purpling nicely, but her crestfallen face made him think Kat had given her an emotional lashing. And he could just imagine the topic.

He knew that Kat was dying to give Jennie all the details of how he'd gone in search of her when she'd left. And though he could only hope that Kat hadn't taken it upon herself to do it for him, there was a good possibility she'd done exactly that. When one of her siblings was threatened, she acted like a mother bear protecting her cub. He loved her even more for her fierce defense of them, but she needed to learn restraint.

Cole's phone rang and drew Ethan's attention.

"It's Patrick," he said and answered. "I'm having dinner with the family. I'll put you on speaker so you can update all of us at once." Cole pressed his speaker button and laid the phone in the middle of the table. "Go ahead, Patrick."

"Hey, y'all," Patrick said and the family said their hellos.

"I have some news on Caldera. He's still a no-show at work, and I haven't been able to locate him, but I did talk with his neighbor. She told me he came to the U.S. after his little sister died in Mexico. Now here's the interesting part. Photos of Hope arranged for the sister to get antibiotics through a local clinic."

"She was one of our clients?" Jennie asked.

"According to the neighbor."

"How did she die?"

"When the family went to pick up the drugs, the clinic claimed the antibiotics had been stolen and she never got her medicine. Caldera says he investigated, and according to him, the drugs were sold in a black-market transaction."

All eyes turned on Jennie.

"I wish I could say it's likely he's wrong, but it's

not uncommon in Mexico for something like this to happen."

She sounded so sad.

"Whenever we get a report of issues with medicine from clients, our first step is to make sure they receive a replacement. Then we ask for a police investigation. Unfortunately, many officers are on the take as well, so the investigations rarely do any good."

"You'd have records if this happened?" Kat asked.

"If his sister was a Photos of Hope client, we'd definitely have a record of working with her. But I wouldn't hold out hope that the family contacted us when the drugs went missing. If they had, we'd have made sure she got the medicine and maybe she'd be alive today."

"If my sister was dying and couldn't get her medicine," Kat said, "I'd get on the phone to Photos of Hope and ask for help."

"Sometimes the families do call, but oftentimes they're just so resigned to the corrupt system that they do nothing." Jennie took a deep breath and let it out slowly. "I'll follow up to see if his family reported the problem."

"Is it possible they did call and someone in your charity dropped the ball?" Patrick asked.

"I hope not, but anything's possible."

"Regardless of what actually happened," Ethan said, "it sounds like Caldera is blaming Photos of Hope, and he could be looking for a way to avenge his sister's death."

"That's my take on it," Patrick replied.

"I think you should put a priority on following up on this." Nods around the table confirmed Ethan's opinion. "We're all in agreement here, Patrick. Keep after this lead."

Cole disconnected the call. "So, what do you think?"

"My heart breaks that another child died." Jennie paused. "But I have to admit to feeling relieved that this may not be about Sotos. Maybe it's just a coincidence that I caught him in a picture."

"Don't get too excited, Jen," Ethan cautioned. "I'm still liking Sotos for all of this. With everything that's happened, it would take a good-size operation to pull this off."

"But if Caldera's a gang member, he'd have his fellow members as a resource." Hope continued to hang in her words.

"I hate to say this, but too many things have happened that don't fit the way a gang member would act on his own." Kat sounded apologetic. "He wouldn't have stopped at ransacking your house or shooting Ashley. He'd have taken valuables for the cash they'd bring. It's a bad sign that nothing was touched."

"Kat's right," Ethan said. "Someone has to be calling the shots. Someone with enough power to make them leave behind a room full of expensive cameras. And our fake detectives were clearly not gang members. The more time I've had to think about how they acted, the more I'm convinced they were real cops. I doubt they work for the local police but Sotos probably has them on the payroll elsewhere."

Cole raised a brow, questioning Ethan.

"I'm not trying to make excuses for what I did, but these guys knew enough to ask for my carry permit. Not something most civilians would think to do. And those fake IDs were flawless."

Ethan's phone rang.

"Derrick," he said, after looking at caller ID. "What's up, bro?"

"My Portland police connection called. The men had cleared out by the time they arrived at the warehouse. Techs are processing the scene now."

Ethan's heart sank at the news. "Maybe we'll get a break and they'll lift a few viable prints."

"Even if they do, I'm sure these guys have gone so far underground, we'll never find them."

Good point, but not one Ethan wanted to focus on. "Keep me informed if you hear anything else." He disconnected.

"What's going on?" Jennie's voice held a nervous tremor.

"The suspects fled the warehouse before the cops arrived," he said and waited for her response.

She didn't say anything but got up and left the room.

Not good, but expected. He didn't think twice, but followed her and found her pacing in the living room.

"This is never going to end, is it?" She stopped and looked at him.

He had to give her an honest answer, but he didn't have to be blunt. "I don't know."

"Once the show opens and I don't display the picture, they could back off."

"Maybe, but as long as they know you have the potential of showing it, then you're in danger."

"So let's just give them the negatives and CD."

"They won't believe you've given them everything. Not after the way you've evaded them so far."

"So you're saying Sotos will be after me for the rest of my life."

Her dejected tone hit him hard. He had to shove his hands in his pockets not to reach out and comfort her. "No, Jen, I didn't say that. We'll come up with a way to make it end."

"Like what?"

"Like once we have more than circumstantial evidence to prove he's behind this, we'll call in the DEA to find a way to bring down Sotos."

"Is that even possible?"

"It's possible."

"Your tone tells me it's not likely though, right?" She stared at him.

He didn't want to continue down a road that wouldn't help them and would only cloud the need to stay focused and vigilant now. "You know what? Speculating about this isn't doing you any good."

Her eyes narrowed and tears formed in the bottomless depths.

"Don't cry, Jen," he said softly.

"I don't want to cry." She looked up at the ceiling. "I thought after all I've seen in life that I could handle anything. But I was wrong. So wrong." Her shoulders started to shake.

He couldn't just stand there and do nothing. He moved closer and brought her chin up with a gentle hand. She avoided his gaze.

"Look at me, honey."

She did, lifting scared and fragile eyes to his.

"You're not alone in this. I'm with you until it's resolved." He smoothed the hair from her face. "Do you hear me? You're not alone."

Her tears intensified, big plump ones sliding down her cheeks and over the darkening bruise.

Not the response he expected. "Aw, man. What'd I say?"

"I've been alone virtually all my life, Ethan." She paused and drew in a breath, her tears slowing. "I don't really know how to believe you'll be around when it counts."

He drew her into his arms. "Do you feel my arms around you?"

"Yes," she whispered.

"Whenever you doubt that I'll be there, remember this and know I'm here for as long as you need me."

She leaned back and looked deep into his eyes. Her eyes melted into warm chocolate, filled with trust and affection, if he read them right. His heart took a tumble, and his pulse eased into high gear. He'd proven that he'd be by her side no matter what, and he should back away. Get out of this room. Go anywhere but deeper into her eyes.

She reached up and trailed a finger along the side of his face, and he caved. He lowered his head and let his lips claim hers. Warm and soft. He felt as if he'd come home for the first time in years. A home that he had no right to claim. The feeling was so unexpected his heart lost track of its beat.

He stifled a wave of emotions and moved back. Setting her away, he took time to catch his breath. Her eyes held confusion, maybe regret and distrust. He should never have kissed her. Everything he'd accomplished in his promise to be there for her had been undone with one simple kiss.

Cole poked his head in the room and nodded at Ethan. "You have a minute or am I interrupting?"

"I was just leaving," Jennie said and fled toward the dining room.

"Everything okay?"

"Just peachy," Ethan answered. "What'd you need?"

"Dani called. She tailed the assistant to a dealer. It appears the dealer is Linda's boyfriend. Dani thinks he could be the guy who paid Linda to leak the news to the press. She wants us to have a little chat with him."

Good. After the way things went with Jennie, Ethan could stand to interrogate a suspect. "I'll tell Kat we're leaving."

"Already did." Cole turned toward the door.

Ethan followed him and caught a glance of Jennie clearing the dining table and talking with Kat. She didn't look up. Maybe she was avoiding him or maybe she just didn't see him. Either way, he'd spend a sleepless night wondering if his kiss had caused irreversible damage between them.

THIRTEEN

In the kitchen with the early-morning sun shining brightly through the window, Jennie finished her call to the Photos of Hope office as she heard the front door open.

"Kat," Ethan called out.

"In the office," Kat yelled back.

He'd arrived right on time to take Jennie to the photo shoot. She was looking forward to losing herself in her work and taking her mind off everything that had been happening, but she wasn't looking forward to spending time in close quarters with Ethan.

Even ten hours later, she could still feel his kiss. The warmth of his lips. The strength in his hold. The affection she thought he was transmitting. She could also feel the sting of his rejection. He'd promised to be there for her, and then like a slap in the face, he'd pulled away without an explanation. Still, she was going to get into his truck, make the ten-minute trip to the photo shoot and pretend nothing had happened between them.

She went to Kat's office to return her cell phone.

She gave a brief nod to Ethan, who perched on the corner of his sister's desk, looking refreshed and too appealing. His hair was still damp above the collar of a crisp blue shirt and he was clean shaven. She wanted to let her eyes linger, but she concentrated on handing the phone to Kat instead.

"Find anything out about Caldera's sister?" Kat asked.

"She was definitely a client of Photos of Hope and she was supposed to get a prescription, but there's no record of a follow-up call from the family."

"That's good, then. Your charity isn't to blame."

"Either way, a child died."

"Caldera may still blame you for that," Ethan added, "and be out for revenge."

"Did you learn anything last night to help confirm that?" Kat asked.

"Maybe. Linda's drug dealer is indeed her boyfriend. He claims he was paid to get Linda to call the newspaper. He didn't know the man, but he has the same tattoo as Munoz and Caldera so I showed him Munoz's picture. He says the payer wasn't him."

"Do you believe him?"

Ethan shrugged. "As much as one can believe a drug dealer. He's meeting with a police sketch artist right now. We'll see what they come up with."

"Sounds like another dead end." Jennie hated how defeated she sounded.

"Don't give up, Jen," Kat offered. "Investigations like these take time and we have your back."

Ethan looked at his watch. "We should get going."

Jennie nodded and went to get her things. Before last night's kiss, Ethan would've been the one to try to cheer her up, but he hadn't said a word. He was probably regretting kissing her and thought it best to keep things professional.

Professional she could do. She met him at the door, and once in the truck, she forced her mind onto the upcoming job. They drove deeper into the West Hills, climbing higher into the area with spectacular views of the city and toward properties with much higher value than Kat's already expensive home.

Before long, Ethan slowed and pulled into the circular driveway of a large historic home. "You wait here. I'll check things out and come back for you."

She wanted to tell him not to bother checking. If one of the cartel members lay in wait, they would surely spot him in this posh neighborhood. Bitsy Standiford's house was likely the safest place for her right now.

A housekeeper dressed in a simple gray uniform pulled open the rich mahogany door. Ethan engaged her in an animated conversation until a car pulled up behind her, and then he raced back toward the truck. He gestured at her to stay put.

She swiveled and looked out the back window. A boxy purple Nissan came to a stop behind her. She let out a breath. Nothing to worry about. It was just Hank Frederic, the reporter assigned to this story.

By the time she'd climbed out to introduce Hank to Ethan, he'd already drawn his gun and faced the car.

"Relax," Jennie yelled. "It's just Hank. He's the reporter."

"Get back in the car, Jen." His words were more of a growl.

"But it's just Hank. You already ran a background check on him."

"He's not alone and could be compromised."

She highly doubted that, but if she complied with his demands, this would end faster. She climbed in and left the door open a crack so she could hear.

"Hands where I can see them," Ethan yelled and slowly approached the passenger side of the car. "Step out of the vehicle nice and slow."

"Hey, man, I don't have any cash, if that's what you're after."

Jennie couldn't believe it. What was *he* doing here?

She pushed open the door. "I know him, Ethan. His name is Wes Mahoney. He's a reporter, too, and we used to work together."

She eased out of the car and gaped at Wes. He wore his usual ratty jeans and scuffed cowboy boots. He was long, lean and thinner than she remembered. He was still ruggedly handsome, but a long scar ran the length of his face from an almost deadly motorcycle accident that occurred when they were dating.

She went toward him, but Ethan kept his gun and focus trained on Wes. "What're you doing here?"

"Relax, man. I'm just hoping to do a story on Jen." He gave her a lazy, knowing smile. "Hey, babe. Good to see you."

She wasn't his babe. They'd started dating soon after she'd broken up with Ethan. Their relationship hadn't survived the brain damage resulting from Wes's crash. He recovered physically, but the trauma changed him. He'd become a thrill-seeking adventurer, and he'd thought Jennie was too staid and uptight for him. They'd no longer had anything in common and had parted friends.

Truth be told, she'd been relieved when they'd broken up. She'd liked Wes, but she finally realized she'd only started dating him to bury the pain of her relationship with Ethan. And after the accident and his refusal to do anything to rein in his new personality, they'd had no real future.

Ethan lowered his gun and faced her. Consternation flashed briefly in his eyes before turning back to Wes and assessing him coldly. But Wes's focus stayed on her and he didn't seem to notice Ethan's study.

A tight smile was all she could manage for either man.

Hank climbed out of the driver's side. "Hey, if I thought you'd try to execute the man, I wouldn't have brought him along."

"Why did you?" Jennie asked, all her distress over another surprise coloring her words.

"Now, babe, don't be so mad." Wes came closer.

"I went to the office to see you, and Hank offered to bring me here."

Ethan ignored Wes and glared at Hank. "Did you tell anyone else about this shoot or that you were meeting Jennie here?" he demanded.

Hank looked so confused by Ethan's over-the-top attitude that Jennie jumped in. "Someone's harassing me, and Ethan wants to make sure no one knows I'm here."

"Sally knows, of course," Hank said. "But other than that I haven't talked with anyone else about it."

"Sally's our editor," Jennie clarified for Ethan who was already turning his focus to Wes.

"Sorry to cause such a problem." Wes slipped an arm around her waist and pulled her in for a hug. "But it sure is good to see you."

She planted her hands on his chest and pushed free. "You shouldn't be here, Wes. I'm working."

"I know. But I wanted to do a feature on you. Kind of a day-in-the-life piece. So I needed to get started on it ASAP."

"Why on earth would you want to do a feature on me?"

He took her elbow and steered her away from the others. "See, here's the thing, babe. I kinda blew my career. You know I lost my way for a while there, but I've been going to counseling, and I really want to get my life back on track."

"Why choose me? There are tons of stories far more interesting and much closer to home."

"I saw the press release for your show in the paper. So I looked you up online. When I saw the controversy over your show, I thought it'd be a great story. Big, bad men trying to hurt little kids will get national play and be picked up by the AP." She knew what he was thinking. If the Associated Press ran his story, it could help him land a job in a time when positions in the newspaper industry were hard to come by.

She didn't need Wes to complicate things right now, but the brain injury that ruined his life wasn't his fault. Plus, she owed him. He'd helped her get her very first job at a newspaper, and without that, she didn't know where she'd be now. And he was the only man she'd dated that she'd ever told about giving up her daughter who hadn't judged her.

"Look." He came closer. "Let's start over, okay? I'm sorry things turned out like they did. We had some good times. Remember?" His eyes cleared, and he smiled sweetly. The smile she'd once fallen for. "Can't you give a guy a break? I won't get in the way. I promise."

She really did want to help him out, but things were so crazy now she couldn't see adding him to the mix. "I don't know, Wes."

"You want me to beg? Fine. I'll beg. Please, Jen. I really need this. You're my last hope." He stabbed his fingers through his thick hair. "I don't know what I'll do if you turn me down. I spent every last dime coming here."

She didn't want to make a decision this quickly, but

Mrs. Standiford was clipping down the driveway, and Jennie didn't want to make a scene.

"You'll stop calling me *babe?*" she asked.

He nodded, his eyes lighting up.

Ethan came over to them. "Is everything okay?"

"Fine," she said, feeling at peace with her decision. "Wes will be joining us to do a story on me."

Wes's fist went up in a victory pump.

"What exactly will that entail?" Ethan asked.

"I'll follow Jennie around for the next few days and take notes." He grinned. "I'll be so quiet you won't even know I'm there."

Ethan scowled and drew Jennie aside. "I need to check Mahoney out before I'll let him do anything beyond covering today's event."

"It's Wes we're talking about here. He's not going to hurt me."

"I won't take any chances."

Jennie glanced at Wes and saw the hopeful look still in his eyes. "I've already said he could do the story."

"If I get the team working on this right away, I should have enough information to clear him by the time you finish here."

Mrs. Standiford was only a few feet away and Jennie didn't want her personal business broadcast in front of a client. "Fine. Check him out."

"What's going on here?" Mrs. Standiford stopped near them, hands on nonexistent hips, and peered at Ethan. "Don't I know you?" she asked him.

"That you do, Mrs. Standiford." Ethan held out his hand and offered her a charming smile. "Ethan Justice."

"Oh, my goodness, of course." She shook his hand. "You're all grown up." She let her eyes rove over him from top to bottom. "All grown up. It feels like yesterday when you and John spent all your free time here. Now he's married, and I have three wonderful grandchildren." She grabbed Ethan's hand and held it out. "Not married, I see."

Jennie didn't like the direction this day was taking. She needed to bring things back to a professional level.

"I'm sorry we're late for our appointment, Mrs. Standiford. We had a bit of a mix-up out here, but we're ready to start the interview if you are."

"*Mrs. Standiford* is my mother-in-law," she said and offered a perfect smile. "Please, everyone call me Bitsy."

Jennie nodded and gestured at Wes. "I hope you don't mind, but Wes will also be joining us. He's a reporter and he's doing a story on my foundation."

Bitsy turned to Wes and looked him over more thoroughly than her intent scouring of Ethan.

Unlike Ethan, Wes warmed to the attention and held out his hand. "My story may be on Jennie, but I'm looking forward to getting to know you, too."

"Then let's get started."

"Shall we?" Wes offered his arm, and Bitsy took it. Wes had always been charming. Too charming.

They headed toward the house and Hank followed them. Jennie went to the truck to retrieve her gadget bag and tripod. She also grabbed her tote bag containing the negatives. She'd packed them since they were leaving directly from here to go to the darkroom, and she wouldn't leave them unprotected in the truck.

Ethan took everything from her. "Guess you have a history with Wes," he said as a statement not a question.

"We worked together in Harlingen," she answered.

Ethan eyed her for a long moment as if he knew there was more to this relationship than work. "I know Texas is a world unto itself, but is it typical for coworkers to call each other *babe?*"

She didn't want to have this conversation with Ethan—with anyone for that matter—and especially not here. She started for the door. "Can we talk about this later?"

He went ahead. "Will we talk about this later?"

Knowing they should stay away from their personal issues, she shrugged and kept walking. Ethan opened the front door, and she went into the entryway, turning in a circle to view the large foyer. She'd done her homework last night on the six-million-dollar home built in the forties and had expected luxury, but she wasn't prepared to see the opulence of this Georgian estate.

"Bitsy has given us permission to shoot the entire estate, which will make a great backdrop for the story." Hank was digging out his notebook from his jacket pocket. "She said since Ethan practically grew up in this house he could show you around while I do the interview. That is, if he wants to."

"Happy to oblige," Ethan answered.

"When you're finished, come find us in the sitting room and we'll wrap things up with some shots of Bitsy." Hank departed.

"Lead on," Jennie said to Ethan and hoped he'd not bring up all the questions about Wes again once they were alone.

"Might as well start in the library. They have an impressive collection of first-edition books." He headed in the opposite direction of Hank.

Jennie traipsed after him, feeling out of her element, but Ethan fit in quite well. He just had an air about him that only came from extreme confidence. He walked with his back straight, his steps powerful and sure. With his casual yet expensive clothes, he looked as if he'd just returned from a laid-back event, socializing with the rich and famous.

And yet, she could also see him coming home to a cozy house, kicking his feet up and letting his kids crawl all over him. That was the more dangerous Ethan. At least, dangerous to her peace of mind.

In the library, Ethan called Kat to start Wes's background check, and Jennie lifted her camera, trying to forget how uncomfortable she felt. The confident world traveler and businesswoman she'd become had disappeared the moment she'd stepped into this house, and the teenager with secondhand clothes and hunger in her stomach emerged. As an adult, she rarely felt this inferior, but since all this had come up in her conversations with Ethan, the feelings lingered in her stomach like a virus. She was sure she looked as uncomfortable as she felt.

Not Ethan, though.

She caught him in her viewfinder as he lounged against the doorjamb and gazed out a window. The night of his parents' anniversary party came to mind. The posh seaside club filled with people from the same social group as Bitsy. Ethan, charming and polite when talking with his parents' friends, oblivious to all the moneyed young women gazing at him. Their eyes occasionally traveling to her. Catching sight of her cheap dress. Scorn or maybe derision taking over.

All the memories of her childhood—hunger, dingy apartments and taunts from other children—made her turn the camera in another direction. If her feelings toward Ethan continued to move her closer to wanting a relationship with him, memories of today would serve as a perfect reminder of one of the many reasons they could never be together.

Dark clouds were building in the distance. Ethan went to retrieve the truck and drive it under the portico. With Jennie's sullen mood, he wasn't looking forward to riding next to her. He figured she was upset over the old boyfriend showing up unannounced. As was he. He hated the way the guy kept looking at her all afternoon. At least he'd quit calling her *babe*.

That had grated on Ethan like heavy-gauge sandpaper, rubbing him raw in seconds. Ethan's past research told him this was the man she'd dated after bailing on him. Then she'd moved to Texas to be near him. Ethan might have known all about the guy before, but he didn't want to meet the man who'd taken his place with Jennie. He'd hoped one of his siblings would've turned up something—anything—he could use to keep Wes away from Jennie, but the guy was clean. Squeaky clean.

Ethan heard voices behind him and glanced back. Jennie, Wes and Hank had exited the house and stood near the door. Jennie and Hank chatted while Wes tapped on his cell phone. He'd had it out all afternoon, sending and receiving texts like a teenage girl. Ethan couldn't help but wonder what was so important in the man's life that he couldn't sit quietly and observe for one afternoon.

Ethan climbed in the truck and the roar of a motorcycle stopped him from closing the door. A high-powered bike raced down the hill and skidded in a wild turn onto the driveway.

"Watch out, Jen," Ethan yelled as he drew his gun, but the bike's engine buried his words. He took off running.

Jennie turned, her eyes wide.

Tires ripped across the concrete, the bike sliding out of control for a moment. Ethan picked up speed but the bike roared up beside Jennie and the driver reached out, snagging the strap on both her bags in one grasp.

The force wrenched her around and sent her spinning. Hank and Wes stood, watching it all unfold.

Jennie lost her balance and teetered until she crumpled onto the cobblestones. Her camera, still hanging from her neck, broke free and flew across the driveway.

With a burst of earsplitting speed, the bike raced off, the engine soon settling into a quiet hum as it disappeared.

Breathless, Ethan reached the top of the drive.

"Are you hurt?" He dropped to his knees and searched Jennie for injury.

"I'm fine." She tried to sit up, but he held her in place.

"We need to make sure you don't have any serious injuries before you move." He looked up at Wes hovering over them as if in shock. "Call 9-1-1."

Ethan saw Hank grab his phone and make the call.

"I'm fine." Jennie pushed against Ethan's hand.

He held firm. "I still want an official confirmation of that before you move."

Their eyes battled it out.

"Fine." Frustration flowed from hers. "My negatives were in the tote bag, Ethan. Now how will I open the show?"

"Let's not worry about that right now."

"How's my camera?" She turned her head, searching.

Just like her to be more concerned about everything but herself. He looked around and spotted it a few feet away.

"If you stay here, I'll get it."

"I won't move."

"Promise?"

"Yes, I promise."

He retrieved the shattered camera, but before he could return, Wes had dropped to his knees and tried to take Jennie's hand. She pulled it free.

That's my girl.

Ethan stopped short. His girl, huh? When had he started thinking like that?

She wasn't his girl. Couldn't be his girl. His brain knew that to be the truth, so why couldn't his heart seem to get the message?

FOURTEEN

In Kat's dining room, Jennie held a cool, damp glass of iced tea against the scrape on her hand. Wes chugged a can of cola as if they'd just found their way out of a desert instead of Bitsy's driveway. Ethan had fussed over her for a few moments, but once she was settled, he went to the kitchen to bring Cole and Kat up to speed on the latest incident.

She hadn't been physically hurt—at least nothing beyond bruising, that small scrape and a considerable burn around her neck from the camera strap—but her emotions had left her one step away from a crying jag. She didn't know how many more setbacks she could take.

"So this is the end of the show, then." Wes settled his can on a coaster and draped a long arm over the chair next to him.

This close she could see the lines near his eyes and the dark circles underneath that seemed permanently etched into his skin. He'd lived life hard since she'd last seen him.

"Is the show over, Jennie?" he asked, and she slid back to the present.

"The pictures are on Kat's disc. I can print from that." She wouldn't be happy with the quality of the photos she turned out, but she was probably the only one who'd notice the difference. Besides, she'd already had time to print over half of the images.

The biggest obstacle right now was convincing Ethan to let her leave this house to work somewhere with a good-quality digital printer and framing equipment. He hadn't said anything, but she could tell after this latest incident that he wanted to lock her in Kat's house until the show.

"That's good, then." Wes studied her for long, uncomfortable moments. "You got something going on with that Ethan dude?"

"No."

He shrugged. "He seems a little possessive so I thought you might be dating or something."

"I think you're mistaking protective for possessive."

"Maybe," he answered, but his eyes said differently.

She was about to ask him to clarify when the Justice trio came into the room. Ethan led the way, an unusual scowl on his face.

He turned the back of a chair to face her then straddled it. "We think it's in your best interest if you stay here until the show opens."

Not surprising that *he* thought that way, but all of them? "We?"

"The three of us." Kat's eyes were more apologetic

than Ethan's unreadable ones. "Whoever's after you has the resources to find you whenever you leave this house. So it's best to keep you here until the show opens."

"I still can't figure out how they could've found me at Bitsy's house. My supervisor and Hank were the only ones who knew the location. Hank said he'd only told Wes, and Sally had no reason to tell anyone."

"You didn't call or email anyone, did you?" Kat asked.

"Oh, no." Her heart sank. "This is all my fault. I checked my work email when I was making the CD for the fake detectives. There was a message from my boss about the shoot." She looked up at Ethan, his expression still blank, so she rushed on to explain. "I know you said not to use email, but I didn't even think about it. It's just a habit. But I know they didn't see my monitor. It was facing the other way." She glanced at each of them. "I'm so, so sorry for putting all of you in danger."

"This isn't your fault, Jen," Ethan said. "If they located you from an email, whether you checked it or not, they'd have to hack your account to actually read the message."

She sighed. "I guess this proves you're right. I should stay here. But what about finishing the photos for the show? You know how I feel about canceling, but if that's what I have to do to not put you all in danger again, then that's what I'll do."

"We're not asking you to do that." Despite Ethan's

blank expression, his tone was tender. "We'll pick up the pictures you've already printed from the darkroom and get all the necessary supplies to print the rest of them right here."

"And what about matting and framing?"

"One of Derrick's friends has a frame shop." Kat's eyes gentled. "He'll come over to teach all of us how to help make the mats, and he'll provide the materials. He'll also bring frame samples with him. You can choose the ones you want and he'll build them at the shop."

They'd thought of everything. What a family. What friends. Were they her friends? Could she call them that? If they were just doing their job, they wouldn't care about the pictures, only her safety. Of course, she could be mistaken and they simply wanted to help the children as much as she did. Regardless, their thoughtfulness warmed her heart.

"I'll need a good-quality printer," she warned, giving them a chance to back out. "And it will be pricey."

"Whatever you need, we'll get it." Ethan's sincerity rang through his words. "Make a list, and everything on it will be here before the end of the day."

He was an amazing man. Sadness over ever having left him hit her hard. She focused on his hands, which were clasping the chair so tightly they'd paled. He'd do whatever it took to help her achieve her goal and still keep her safe. She wanted to empty the room of all others. Let him hold her as he had that one summer of her life when she'd felt cherished and safe.

"Jen," he said.

She was such a dope for constantly heading down that path. "I'll start on the list right away."

"I'll get some paper," Kat offered.

To keep her eyes off Ethan, Jennie looked the other way. She caught Wes studying her. "You may want to call off your story, Wes. Sitting in this house isn't going to be too exciting."

"I'll just have to change my slant. The way this family has come to your rescue so you can help the kids will make a great human-interest piece, too." He smiled at her. "Plus I can pitch in and you'll have one more person to help get the pictures ready."

"Thanks, Wes." Maybe he really had changed and could now show some responsibility.

Kat came back with a pad and pen.

"Okay, then." Jennie smiled. "Will everyone quit looking at me and go do something so I can think?"

Kat laughed. "C'mon, I'll make lunch and you all can watch me instead."

"Now, that I'm up for," Wes answered and shot to his feet, following all of them into the kitchen.

Jennie started the list, working for nearly an hour and using her laptop to check model numbers on the internet as she went. At some point, Kat placed a sandwich, chips and soda next to her and, other than a squeeze on the shoulder, said not a word.

Satisfied she hadn't forgotten a thing, Jennie went to the kitchen to deliver the list. She walked in on Wes telling a story about a trip he'd taken with her to

Sauvie Island for the annual corn maze. The memories of a fun day made her smile.

It had been a great day at the beginning of their relationship. A day filled with laughter and promise of a happy future. Wes had grown up in a tough environment, too, and had clawed his way out of poverty. In that respect, she'd felt more at ease with him than with Ethan. Her relationship with Ethan had held excitement. Love only found in fairy tales. Dreams for an amazing future. It was different with Wes. Less intense, more affection and contentment than anything. Companionship, she supposed.

She watched his animated face, looking so reminiscent of when they'd first met. She didn't have a clue why he'd decided to tell this particular story, but everyone laughed when he admitted how he'd gotten lost and she'd had to get a staff member to find him.

"Remember, Jen?" He caught her eye, and she saw that he remembered far more than that.

"Yes." She smiled.

"You done with the list?" Ethan jumped in, his voice gruff.

She held it up.

"I'm the gofer." Cole took the paper and ran a finger down it. "I don't need to understand any of this, right? I just have to hand this to the guy at the store you recommended and he'll know what it means."

Jennie gave him a reassuring smile. "I was thorough, but if they have any questions you can call me."

"Then I'm off." He headed for the door.

"I'll walk you out," Ethan said and followed him.

Jennie turned to Kat. "Thanks for the lunch. Is it okay if I use the living room to work on editing pictures from today's shoot?"

Kat nodded. "I'll be here doing the dishes and getting something together for dinner tonight. Let me know if I can do anything to help."

If Kat hadn't warned her off Ethan, Jennie would never know by Kat's cordial behavior that she didn't like what was going on between the two of them.

Jennie took her laptop to the living room and settled on the sofa to edit Bitsy's photos. Despite the attack at the end of the shoot, Jennie still had a five-o'clock deadline to meet. Her camera was toast, but fortunately, her memory card had survived the crash. She went to work and knocked out the edits in less than an hour.

She accessed an online backup site and copied all of her pictures. After the manhandling this afternoon, she was taking no chances that something like this could happen again and the CD for the show could be damaged or destroyed.

Ethan returned from seeing Cole out, but didn't stop to talk to her. She opened the first photo of Marisol and smiled at the little urchin who'd captured her heart like so many of these children had. Jennie wanted to keep helping them—that was a given—but after everything that had happened in the past few days, she realized she wanted more. Much more. She didn't want to be alone any longer.

She sighed and went back to her screen, viewed, cropped and enhanced photo after photo. At some point, Dani arrived and announced that the sketch artist had finished with Linda's drug-dealer boyfriend and had distributed his drawing to the rank and file. At first, it had cast a pall over the group, but soon warm conversation drifted from the kitchen.

At a boisterous outburst of laughter, Jennie stopped to listen. It was nice knowing others were nearby rather than her usual solitary existence at home. But here she was in the living room, still an outsider longing for a family like the Justice family. Didn't matter. They belonged in the same dream as having a husband and children of her own.

A dream, no matter how much she now knew she wanted, she couldn't see anywhere in her future.

Ethan stretched his lower back from leaning over the dining room table. Wes, Kat, Dani, Cole and he had been cutting mats all afternoon in the colors and dimensions Jennie had specified. At least, Wes was supposed to be working on the mats.

After halfheartedly cutting out a few sloppy ones, he'd claimed this kind of work didn't suit him. But, he'd added, with his experience as a reporter, he could help Jennie choose the best pictures to print. And without a backward glance, he'd slunk off to the living room.

Okay, maybe not slunk, but he'd gone to the living room, and Ethan had wanted to follow. To march up to him and tell him to leave Jennie alone to do her work. But he'd held his tongue. Jennie was a big girl. If she couldn't work with Wes in there, she'd send him packing.

She hadn't, though. Not in three hours. Three hours while all sorts of things drifted through Ethan's mind. At times, their voices were hushed, other times raised and peppered with laughter. Now was one of those laughter-filled times, and Ethan couldn't take it anymore.

He took a few steps toward the door and stopped when he spotted Jennie, eyes alight with amusement, listening to Wes's story. Ethan fisted his hands. How could he be reacting like this to Wes? Jennie wasn't interested in him. She'd made that clear. Even if she was, it wouldn't matter. Ethan had no claim to her.

She reached out and squeezed Wes's arm, her face tipped up, shining with happiness. That's it. That's what was bothering him. She used to look at him that way. Now, when their eyes met, he saw only pain, maybe regret, and he wanted to go back to when they shared moments like this. It was time for them to talk. Beyond time.

He took a step.

"Don't go in there." Kat laid a hand on his arm and gave him a warning look.

He returned her look with an arched brow.

"In the kitchen." She didn't wait for his agreement to follow but headed that direction.

Ethan took one last look into the living room and followed Kat.

"You're playing with fire." Kat poured a cup of coffee. "And you're the one who's gonna get burned again."

"What are you talking about?" Ethan slid onto a stool.

"Please. I see the way you're looking at Jennie. It's that summer all over again. And you'll be the one left behind to pick up the pieces." She blew on the cup and eyed him over the rim.

"First of all, nosy sister of mine, I am not looking at Jennie in any special way."

Kat snorted. "Right."

"And even if I was, what makes you so certain she'd leave again?"

"Because she still hasn't worked out whatever made her bail the first time."

"And how do you know that?"

"I talked to her about it."

"You what?" He shot up and planted his hands on the counter. "You had no business butting in here, Kat."

"I love you, Ethan, and I'm not going to stand around and watch you get hurt again," she said with unwelcome frankness. "In case you've forgotten, which I can't imagine you could have, she practically destroyed you last time."

He wanted to throttle his sister. Her heart was good—she just stuck her nose in areas she shouldn't, and his love life, or lack thereof, was one of those areas she couldn't seem to stay away from.

He went to her and clasped her shoulders, looking down on her until she raised her head to meet his gaze. "I'm touched that you want to protect me, Kat. But you can't always worry about me or anyone else in the family getting hurt." He leaned forward and kissed her forehead.

"Just try to look at this with open eyes, okay?"

He laughed. "You really don't know when to give up, do you?"

"Some things are worth not giving up on." She raised her coffee in a mock toast and went to the dining room.

Ethan's phone chimed and he answered the call from Derrick.

"They found our fake detectives," Derrick said.

"Where? Are they talking?"

"Down by the river and no." Derrick paused and Ethan heard him draw in a breath. "The gunshots through the backs of their heads guarantee neither of them will be saying anything again."

Jennie went to the kitchen to get a bottle of water. She found Ethan sitting at the bar, talking on the phone. His eyes narrowed, but when he caught sight of her, they warmed. Not to the cool, formal mood of late, but to something heated and compelling, drawing her closer and making her want to smooth away the furrow in his forehead. The last thing she should do.

She grabbed the water from the refrigerator then headed for the door before she did or said something dumb.

"Jen, wait," he called out.

"Everything okay?" she asked while swimming through the haze of feelings bombarding her.

"That was Derrick. The police found the fake detectives. They were murdered."

"They're coming for me next, aren't they?" She felt panic climb up with each word.

Ethan crossed to her. "We won't let them get to you, Jen."

"After everything that's happened, I'm not sure I believe you can stop them."

"Don't worry." He smiled but she could see it was forced. "They have no idea where you are and can't find you. As long as you do what we say and stay here, you're safe."

She let the intensity of his gaze settle over her frayed nerves. "So why the tense face, then?"

"Can we talk?"

"This doesn't sound good." She searched for the meaning behind his words.

"Why don't we go sit in the living room?"

"You're scaring me, Ethan."

"Nothing to be afraid of." He stood and gestured toward the other room.

She went through the dining room, not giving any attention to the group working around the table.

"Out." Ethan cast a harsh glare at Wes, who was peering at his cell phone.

Wes's head lifted, defiance in his eyes. He stared at Ethan for a long moment then shrugged. "I'll be in the next room if you need me," he said to Jennie.

Ethan fisted his hands and watched Wes leave.

"Was that necessary?" Jennie asked.

"I don't like him, Jen."

"I can see that." She sat on the sofa. "But he's done nothing to deserve such harsh treatment."

"You're right." He crossed the room and sat next to her. "It's just—" He looked away.

"Just what?"

"I don't know, all right?" His voice raised and she couldn't decipher the sudden change in him. She waited to speak until she could see his face.

"I don't know." He spoke softly now and looked at her. "But he shouldn't be here with you." He shook his head. "He just shouldn't."

"This is what you wanted to talk to me about?"

He took a deep breath. "No. I actually wanted to tell you about what happened after you left me. What I did."

"Okay." The tension in her own voice left her unsettled.

"I tried to find you. I started at your work, but you'd quit. Then your college, but you'd moved and changed schools. It took me almost a year of searching in my spare time before I discovered you'd moved to Texas."

Her mouth dropped open. "You were still looking for me then?"

His expression grew uneasy, but he continued. "I thought you were my soul mate, Jen. I thought if I could just talk to you, I could convince you to change your mind."

The pain in his voice had her reaching out and taking his hand. "I'm so sorry, Ethan. I never imagined you'd keep looking for me."

"Maybe I kept looking because you were so hard to find and I didn't want to give up. Or I was just being stubborn." He gave a wry laugh. "Tracking you down is what got me interested in joining the FBI."

"That's good, I guess."

"Following your trail was as difficult as some of my cases at the bureau. It wasn't until I tracked you back to Springbrook that—"

"You went to Springbrook?" Her voice skyrocketed.

"Yes."

She stifled a gasp. He'd found the town where she'd gotten pregnant. A town small enough that people would remember an unwed mother. Especially an unwed mother whose father had worked odd jobs for a little cash from many of the townspeople. But she had to hear him say it so she could finally put to rest the hope of being with him.

"And what did you find there?" she asked, almost breathless.

"The biggest thing, I guess, is that you had a baby and gave her up for adoption."

She waited for his face to tighten with disgust, but it didn't change at all. Maybe he was too well mannered to tell her how he felt. "And once you found out about the baby, that's when you stopped looking, right?"

"No, why would you think that?"

"Because I'd done the one thing you couldn't abide."

He stared at her, clearly baffled.

He was going to make her be the one to say it. "You told me it was unthinkable for a mother to give away her child. You hated your mother and said you'd never forgive her for giving you up. So I knew you'd feel the same way about me."

He just looked at her. His expression unreadable. Time ticked by. She wanted to bolt but she'd done enough running where he was concerned. It was time to sit and hear him out.

"I hadn't thought of it that way, Jen," he finally said. "I guess if you'd told me about the baby when we first met, I might not have given you the time of day."

She heard something in his voice that gave her hope, but maybe it was just her own optimism tinting his tone. She had to know.

"But?" she asked and held her breath again.

"But I know you, Jen. And I know your heart." He covered her hand with his and squeezed. "I knew it back then, too, and when I found out about your daughter, I never questioned your decision. If you gave her up, I know it was because you loved her and felt it was in her best interest."

She was too shocked to speak.

"In fact, you helped me reconcile with my birth mother," he went on. "When I was growing up, my adoptive parents always said my mom gave me up out of love. But I never felt like that was true. When I saw what you did, I finally got it, and I went to see her."

"And?" Jennie asked, now more interested in this than in her own story.

"We have a relationship."

"You have a relationship with your birth mother." She said it aloud to fully grasp the change in him.

"You sound so surprised."

"From all you used to say about her, I didn't think your feelings would ever change."

He studied her with probing eyes, digging so deep she felt as if everything in her life was open for him to see. She couldn't stand the intensity. She jumped up and went to stand at the fireplace. She heard him get up and follow then felt him right behind her.

He put his hands on her shoulders. "Did you leave because you didn't think you could tell me about the baby?"

"I thought after you knew I gave Natalie away, you'd hate me, too. Once I realized you wanted our relationship to continue past the summer, I was sure the truth would come out eventually. I didn't want to be around when that happened." It felt so good finally to admit it.

"So it was my fault." His words came out in a whisper. "If I hadn't been so stubborn, you might not have ended things."

She turned. "I'm the one at fault. I should have told

you, but I was afraid you'd judge me just like the people in my church did." She shook her head. "They'd always preached forgiveness for any sin, but then I got pregnant and they turned their backs on me. I couldn't stand to see you do the same thing."

"I'm so sorry, Jen." There was a slight tremor in his voice and sadness. Lots of sadness.

"You have nothing to apologize for."

"Yes, I do. I was so closed-minded that you felt you couldn't share this with me."

"You were young and had no idea I was hiding this. It was my decision to break up with you. You had nothing to do with it."

"That's what your father said, too, but—"

"You went to see my father?"

"Yes."

"Where?"

"In Seaside."

This couldn't be happening. She felt physically sick to her stomach. Sure, she'd told him about how she'd lived when she'd known him, but she didn't want to think of him seeing the deplorable conditions firsthand. And he'd walked right into the mess. Right into the ratty apartment she'd gone home to at night after their dates.

He'd seen the filth and the hopelessness she'd endured until she could move out and support herself. The squalor her father had lived in until a few years ago when he'd died from a heart attack in the middle of the night.

And now, now he knew the real Jennie that no one knew. The person she'd been trying to hide since she understood what the word *poverty* meant, thanks to unfeeling kids in the second grade.

He worked the muscles in his jaw, his eyes unreadable. She knew he was preparing to tell her that, though he'd kissed her last night, their lives were so different that they weren't compatible.

Well, she'd beat him to the punch.

She straightened her shoulders. "You had no right to go there, Ethan. If I'd wanted you to meet my father, I would've introduced you."

Instead of backing off as she'd hoped, he watched her until his eyes turned sharp and piercing. "You're doing it again, aren't you?"

"I don't know what you mean."

"Yes, you do. You didn't leave me because of the baby. You left because of how you feel about yourself. The way you grew up makes you think less of yourself."

He took a step closer, and she backed up.

"Have you ever tried to contact your daughter?"

"No."

"Why not?"

"I wouldn't know where to begin."

He arched a brow. "If you used an agency that would be the first place to start."

"I didn't use an agency."

"Then how did you arrange the adoption?"

"A local teacher who couldn't have children adopted her."

"Do you remember her name?"

"Why all the questions? It's not like we're going to go looking for her."

"Why not? Because you know she'll be easy to find and then you'll have to face your past?"

"No," she said, though he was speaking the truth. She could look up Natalie's parents anytime she wanted and they'd let her meet Natalie. At least, that's what they'd once promised.

"You really don't want to talk to her, do you, Jen?"

She shrugged.

"You haven't looked for her because you're sure she'll reject you. You don't think you're worthy of love. Giving her up confirms it in your mind and lets the guilt cover up everything else. Helping the kids in Photos of Hope lets you atone for the condemnation, and that's why you're so driven to support them."

She crossed her arms and started to walk away.

"This is it again, isn't it, Jen? You're putting up that wall. Whenever we talk about your past, you change. The incredible woman I've gotten to know again turns into the girl you told me about the other day. The one who didn't fit in or belong anywhere, and you raise the wall so no one can reject you again." He reached out to touch her cheek, and she jerked back. "Let your guard down, Jen. You don't always have to be so tough."

Yes, she did, or she'd find herself really letting go of her past. Forgetting about all the pain of growing up so poor. The ridicule. The heartache. The loss. And then what? Then she might begin to believe a relationship with a man was possible—maybe with a man as wonderful as Ethan—and she'd just open her heart for more rejection.

"I'm not having this discussion with you." She left the room before she caved, before she let this incredible man hold her again and give her hope. And before she made the second biggest mistake ever. Letting him back into her life.

FIFTEEN

Ethan went straight to the dining room, grabbed Cole by the arm and dragged him outside. The cool night air soaked through his shirt and sent a chill over his body. But he didn't care. He wasn't going back inside for a jacket.

"I need you to do something for me," he said after Cole closed the door.

"Okay." Cole's tone was wary.

"Jennie had a baby girl when she was sixteen and gave her up for adoption." Ethan waited for a reaction to this news, but Cole didn't react at all. "I need you to track down this girl ASAP and find out if she wants to meet Jennie. The daughter's name is Natalie and she was placed for adoption with one of Jennie's teachers in Springbrook."

"Aw, man, what're you doing?" Cole asked. "This is something for Jennie to do, not you."

"But she won't do it, so I have to."

"If she won't do it then she doesn't want it done."

"You don't understand. She uses her guilt over giving up the baby to confirm she's unlovable."

"You lost me there."

"She grew up poor and the message she got is that she's not as good as other people. Then she has a baby and lets the guilt over giving up the baby convince her that she's right, she's worthless. But that's a heavy thing to live under so she helps the children to feel better about herself."

"That's pretty deep, bro. Are you sure you're not reading something into this that's not there?"

"I don't know. Maybe. But I have to do this. It's an area I can fix by bringing them together." Ethan heard the desperation in his tone and he wondered for a moment if he was doing the right thing.

"And what if the daughter doesn't want to meet Jennie?"

"Then we'll deal with that if it happens."

Cole raised an eyebrow.

"What?" Ethan asked.

"You're sure you want to do this?" Cole narrowed his eyes. "Because I can see it going totally wrong."

Cole was a wise man, but Ethan didn't think he was right on this one. "Just start the search. I'll deal with the fallout if there is any."

Jennie was tired. Weary to the bone. From the work. From the stress. From her talk with Ethan.

Especially from that.

She rose from her computer and stretched. She turned to listen to the conversation and good-natured ribbing in the dining room while the Justices worked on mats for her photos.

As an only child, she'd missed the camaraderie and discord shared by siblings. Even now, she continued to seclude herself in the living room while the family interacted. She'd told herself it was so she could concentrate, but in reality, she was beginning to think Ethan was right. She didn't think she deserved a family to call her own so she didn't want to see what she was missing.

She glanced at Wes softly snoring on the sofa. She fit in with him, not the Justice family. Dumb thinking, she knew, but that was how she felt, deep inside, anyway. As she listened to the brothers and sisters' down-to-earth conversation, she felt even dumber for believing the lies of her past. These were regular people with regular lives. Not the society mavens she kept seeing in her head who'd look down on her poor background.

So put it aside, Jennie. Go join in for a while.

For once, she listened to her brain, not her heart, and with one last glance at Wes, she headed to the dining room. Ethan stood at the end of the table, Cole at the other end, black-and-white mats in front of them. Dani and Kat sat next to each other on the side, both working on one large mat.

All looked up at her when she entered the room.

"Decided to slum it, huh?" Dani joked.

Not hardly. "Just thought I'd take a break and see how you all are doing."

Cole's phone chimed.

"Patrick." Cole pressed a button on the phone. "You're on speaker. What's new?"

"I located Caldera's brother. Caldera's not after your client."

"Explain," Ethan said, and Jennie could hear excitement in his tone.

"Remember I said Caldera investigated the missing medication for his sister? Well, he thinks Sotos was behind it, and he knew if he tried to have Sotos arrested for it, Sotos would have him killed. So Caldera came to the U.S. to figure out how Sotos was getting the drugs from this end. He went to work for the charity to learn the operation and find a way to get back at Sotos."

"So he's not out to get the charity or Jennie, but Sotos," Kat mumbled as if talking to herself.

"And that could mean Munoz is working with his cousin and not Sotos." Relief started building in Jennie's heart.

"How would that explain them trying to get the picture?" Ethan asked, while his eyes told Jennie not to get her hopes up so fast.

"Since Munoz is local, I think Sotos hired him to break into the gallery and obtain the photo," Patrick said, "then leave a message to scare off Jennie. But once he saw what the photo contained he figured he could use it to get back at Sotos."

"Sounds possible." Ethan's expression was unreadable. "We won't know until we can talk to Caldera or Munoz."

"I'll keep after Caldera. See if I can find him."

"Thanks, Patrick," Cole said. "We owe you one."

"I like the sound of that." Patrick laughed and ended the call.

Ethan turned to Kat. "Can you put some pressure on your friends at the P.P.B. to find Munoz?"

"Sure."

"I'll check back with Jack to see if his contact at the DEA has gotten anywhere." He glanced at Jennie. "Maybe we'll finally get some good news on this end."

"I'm heading out unless you need me for anything else." Cole picked up his phone. "I need my sleep to survive Madeline duty tomorrow."

"More like your beauty sleep." Ethan quirked a brow and Jennie couldn't help but smile at how much possible good news had changed the atmosphere here.

"Come down here and say that." Cole cast a mock glare at Ethan.

Kat rolled her eyes. "Do I need to separate you boys?"

"*Boys* is right," Dani mumbled.

"Hey, now." Ethan held up a hand and met Jennie's gaze. "You're gonna give Jennie the wrong impression about us."

Kat rolled her eyes. "Like she doesn't know all about you two already."

Everyone looked at Jennie to see what she'd say, but she couldn't think of a thing.

The doorbell rang, and she jumped.

"That's most likely Stephen back with the frames." Ethan gave her a reassuring smile. "You should go into the kitchen until I'm sure."

After her earlier talk with Ethan, she'd chosen framing materials and Stephen had gone back to his shop a few hours ago to start working on them. She was eager to see his work, but she complied and went to the kitchen.

A few minutes later, Kat poked her head in. "It is Stephen. He's finished quite a few of the pictures."

"I'm looking forward to seeing them."

"I've already picked out my favorite." She curled her finger. "C'mon, I want to show you which one I chose."

Jennie followed Kat to the dining room. The family had already carried in stacks of framed photos and leaned them against the walls. Cole and Dani joined them with more pictures then stood viewing them.

Jennie went closer to inspect the work. Perfectly mitered corners. Quality materials that only a true artisan would use.

"This is the last of them." Stephen entered the room, followed by Ethan, each carrying pictures.

"I can't believe you finished these so fast," Jennie exclaimed.

"I had my staff stay late."

"Make sure you add their labor to the bill for the materials," Jennie added.

"There's no charge. We're all happy to volunteer our time to the project."

She looked up. "At least let me pay for the materials."

"I'm good with a charitable-donation form."

She felt tears forming from his kindness. "Thank you, Stephen." She looked at each of the Justices. "And thank you to all of you, too. You're a blessing to these children."

Ethan came up to her. "We're the ones who've been blessed by helping."

She looked into his eyes and knew he spoke the truth. Had he spoken the truth earlier, too? Was she living under condemnation she didn't deserve? Could she change her life if only she tried? His eyes seemed to say she could.

"Well, I'll be taking off, then," Stephen said and headed for the door.

"I'll walk out with you." Cole waved good-night, and the two of them left.

"This is the picture I wanted you to see, Jen." Kat lifted one of the larger photos onto the table.

Jennie joined her. "Stephen is very good at what he does. The framing is amazing."

"I can't seem to take my eyes off it." Kat studied the picture. "It's like the richness of the frame further emphasizes the girl's poverty."

Jennie stroked her fingers down the wood frame. "That's what I was going for when I chose the material."

Kat sniffed and moved back. "Working on these pictures all day has made me weepy."

"Don't cry, little sis." Ethan wrapped his arm around Kat. "You know Dani. She'll be sobbing right along with you."

"I can't help it." Kat looked up at him, her sisterly love shining in her eyes. "Seeing this makes me think about life before my adoption. It's like I'm that girl in the picture and the frame is Mom and Dad." She paused and breathed deep. "They were rich like the frame—with money, yes, but more so with love. They circled their arms around me just like this frame and loved me when no one else did." She started crying in earnest.

Dani dug in her purse, handed a tissue to Kat, then dabbed at her own eyes.

"See, I told you, you'd get Dani going," Ethan said in a joking tone, but his voice had choked up, as well.

Jennie struggled hard not to cry with them and looked at the picture. Had she always chosen the frames she did because she wanted to put a protective circle of love around these children and give them what she never had? Or was it simply an aesthetic thing? Was Ethan right? Had she been trying to make up for feeling unlovable?

Kat transferred her attention to Jennie. "You're an amazing person, Jennie. Doing all of this for these children, even risking your own life for them. When this is all over I'd like to talk to you about our church getting involved with Photos of Hope."

"Thanks, Kat." Jennie's heart warmed, and for the first time ever, she felt as if these people surrounding her accepted her. No matter her past. No matter her decision to give up her daughter. They didn't care about her past. They'd all had to overcome tough beginnings in life as she had. The only difference was that they'd had the love of wonderful parents to help them, where her father had been part of the problem.

She thought back to a sermon she'd clung to until members of her church shunned her for getting pregnant. The pastor had said that no matter the flaws of earthly parents, we have a heavenly Father, who loves us. And though He allows hurt and pain in our lives, He doesn't waste it.

This paralleled something she'd recently read. That where your misery has been, that's where your ministry will be. She'd used her past misery to help these children.

But was the misery all in the past? Not if what Ethan said was true and she kept thinking that she was unworthy of love. That she was less than everything God wanted her to be.

She had to let her past go. Accept that she'd gone through a difficult childhood. Without her past, she may not be helping these children.

She turned away and closed her eyes.

Father, thank You for everything in my life. I hated my childhood, but now I can see how it has allowed me to help all of these children. Even if I have been doing it for the wrong reasons. Now I have to ask, am

I letting my past cloud my decisions? If I am, please show it to me and help me let go of this once and for all. Let me move on with life and live it open to any and all new experiences You have for me. And, Father, if it is Your will, once this is all over, let me reconnect with my daughter.

"Jen." Ethan laid a hand on her shoulder. "You okay?"

She smiled up at him and nodded. When their eyes met, she knew with certainty that she cared about this man. Maybe she was in love with him again. Maybe she'd never really stopped loving him.

Kat's phone rang, startling them both.

"It's Detective Tilden." With a meaningful look at Ethan, Kat answered and left the room.

The mood changed as if a streak of lightning had flashed fear into the room. Jennie wouldn't let go of her peace, though. She'd waited too long to feel this way. No matter what Kat learned, Jennie finally had hope.

Instead of standing around waiting for the news from Kat, they went back to work on the mats. Ethan kept an eye on Jennie, pleased to see her more light-hearted. He didn't know what had occurred to make that happen, but he was thankful.

Wes stumbled into the room, scratching his head. "Sorry. I must've dozed off." He looked around. "Wow, y'all have been busy."

"We're just finishing up for the evening." Jennie

smiled at him. "There's nothing left to do here, so you should go get a good night's sleep."

He stretched. "I'd love to, but I'll need a ride."

"Dani." Ethan pleaded with his eyes. "Can you take Wes to his hotel?"

She glanced at her watch. "My shift with Madeline's in an hour. Derrick will be ticked off if I'm late."

"He can wait."

She looked as if she were about to argue so Ethan stepped up to her. "I'll make it worth your while," he whispered. "You can have your choice of assignments next time."

A cat-that-ate-the-canary smile slid across her face, and she gave a clipped nod before turning to Wes. "Ready to go?"

He nodded. "Sorry I was so lame tonight, Jen. Guess it's the change in time zones. I'll be more help tomorrow, and we can get going on that article."

"Sounds good," Jennie answered.

"I have a rental car. Should I just come back here in the morning, then?"

"No," Ethan said, so forcefully it made Wes jump. "It's better if one of us picks you up. We can't risk anyone following you here."

Wes saluted. "Got it."

Ethan waited for Wes to try to hug Jennie goodnight, but the guy headed out with Dani. Maybe Ethan had been too hard on him. If Jennie had once dated him, he had to have some redeeming qualities.

After the door closed, Jennie faced Ethan. "I'm

sorry he's an additional concern for you when you already have so much on your plate."

Ethan opened his mouth to say "no problem," but he'd be lying so he closed it.

"The last few years have really been hard on him," Jennie went on while she sliced the corners of a blue mat. "He was in a motorcycle accident and sustained a head injury. He lost all ability to filter his emotions and ended up turning into an adrenaline junkie. He didn't want a boring, predictable life, so that's why we broke up." She smiled and flipped the mat. "Sounds like he's finally realized he was throwing his life away, and with counseling, he's back on track."

Ethan felt like a heel for being so tough on the guy.

Kat returned, a broad smile on her face. "They've found Munoz. He admitted to destroying the gallery, tailing Jennie on the train and trashing her house. But he denies having anything to do with the attempt on Ashley's life or the incident at the photo shoot."

"Typical move," Ethan said. "Cop to the lesser charges to make them think he's cooperating."

"Actually, Tilden thinks Munoz is on the up-and-up."

"He say why?" Ethan pulled out a chair and straddled it.

Kat sat next to him. "Munoz claims someone from the Sotos organization contacted him and told him Sotos wanted a picture destroyed. He didn't say what was in the picture, just to retrieve it along with the negatives and digital copies." She looked at Jennie.

"You're not going to like this part, but once he was sure he had everything, he was supposed to kill you."

Jennie shrugged. "It's not like it's a surprise, but I don't like having it confirmed."

"Here's where it gets interesting," Kat added. "Munoz says after he took the negatives from your house, he had the pictures printed. He figured if Sotos was so desperate for the pictures, he had something big to hide. When he saw the one of Sotos, he sent it to Caldera, who identified the other man in the picture."

"Who is he?" Jennie sounded breathless with anticipation.

"Antonio Maceno, a high-ranking Mexican law-enforcement official. Munoz thinks the guy's on Sotos's payroll and Sotos didn't want anyone to find out or he'd lose a valuable asset."

Finally, they knew what this was about. Ethan felt the excitement build in his gut. "A great motive for wanting to keep Jennie from displaying the picture."

"So how was Munoz going to use the photo?" Jennie asked as she dropped onto a chair.

"If the alliance between Sotos and Maceno didn't come out in the gallery opening, he'd give the negatives to the DEA, hoping they'd bring down Sotos, thus avenging his cousin's death."

"Finally, we know what this is all about." Jennie's words echoed Ethan's thoughts.

"One thing I can't figure out, though," Kat said. "How did Sotos know about the picture in the first place? I mean, the exhibit hasn't opened yet and it's not like you know him."

"Good question," Jennie agreed. "I suppose he could have seen me that day, but if he did, why wait so long to try to get the picture back?"

Ethan was just as curious, but he wasn't going to waste any time searching out an answer right now. His number one priority was to make sure Jennie stayed safe. And now that they were certain a ruthless killer like Sotos was behind these attacks, they needed to make sure Sotos didn't find Jennie and end her life.

SIXTEEN

Yawning, Jennie reached for her pajamas draped across the bed in Kat's guest room. She couldn't wait to change clothes and sink into the softness of the pillow-top mattress. She switched off the overhead lamp and crossed the room. As she passed the window, a rustling sound outside caught her attention. She peeked through the blinds.

The inky-black night thick with clouds gave her little to see. Not that there was likely anything to see. It'd been so quiet since everyone had gone home that each creak and groan sent her imagination into overdrive.

She held her breath and listened. There it was again. A sound as if someone was sneaking through the shrubs alongside the house. Could be a cat or dog, but they wouldn't make this much noise, would they?

Fear inching up her back, she ran to the hallway and toward Kat's room to wake her. Kat was already standing there, gun drawn and eyes watchful.

"I think someone's outside." Jennie ran her hands up and down her arms as if she could still her fear.

"I'm on my way to check it out." Kat motioned

down the hall. "You go back to your room and call Ethan. Tell him what's going on."

That meant she'd be alone. "But I—"

"No buts, Jennie. Do as I say." Kat used her cop stare, and Jennie knew better than to argue.

Heading down the hall, she tried to stem her anxiety. Though not Ethan's blood relative, Kat had sounded just like him. In control and prepared.

She'd take care of her, wouldn't she?

Jennie stopped outside her door and watched Kat descend the stairs. Gun outstretched, she inched down them like a stalking cat. When she disappeared from view, Jennie went into the bedroom. She grabbed her cell off the nightstand and dialed Ethan.

"What's wrong?" His voice was both sleepy and alert at the same time.

She went to the window and peeked out. "There's someone prowling around outside."

He hissed out a breath. "Where are you?"

"In my room."

"And Kat?"

"She went outside to check."

"Stay where you are until I get there." She could hear him rushing around, maybe getting dressed. "Stay away from the window. Understand?"

"Yes." She backed away and leaned against the wall.

"Jen?"

"Yeah."

"Promise me you won't go outside."

"I just said I understand."

"Yeah, but that was me telling you what to do, and sometimes you balk at being told what to do, so this is me asking."

Despite the tension, she laughed. "I'll stay inside."

"And away from the window," he added. "Call 9-1-1 when we hang up, okay?"

"Okay." Just hearing his voice was easing her fear, and knowing he'd soon be here helped even more.

"I'll be there in twenty minutes tops." He disconnected.

Twenty minutes? A lot could happen in twenty minutes. A member of the Sotos Cartel could easily kill her and Kat in twenty minutes. Or if not kill, seriously maim them.

Terror took a firm hold and she backed toward the bed. She sat and dialed.

"Nine-one-one, what's your emergency?"

"Someone's outside the house. I think he's trying to get in. I'm staying at a friend's house. Oh, my gosh! What's the address?" Panic raced up her spine.

"Calm down and think."

Jennie tried to picture the bright silver numbers on the blue siding that she'd passed several times. She rattled off the address.

"Good," the operator said.

A crash then a thump sounded outside.

"Kat. Oh, no!"

Please, God. Please!

"Ma'am, is someone hurt?"

"I'm not sure. My friend went out to check. She used to be a cop."

"How about you? Are you someplace safe?"

Was she safe? Not if Kat was incapacitated, she wasn't. But she wasn't sure anyone had gotten to Kat.

The front door smashed against the wall. She heard someone rushing through the downstairs. Moving at a fast clip. Maybe more than one person. Racing. No regard for anything in their path, if the crashing sounds were any indication.

What should she do? Ethan didn't say what to do if someone came into the house.

Oh, God. Oh, God. Please help me.

She kept her eyes on the door. Heard a whooshing sound then saw a flash of light in the space below. The caustic smell of smoke mixed with gasoline followed. She ran to the door. Cracked it open and peered into the hallway. A dark figure darted out the front door, illuminated by bright orange flames licking greedily up the stairs.

She had to get out of there, but how? The stairs weren't an option. The window. But what if that's what they wanted—to smoke her out and shoot her? Did it matter? She'd die if she stayed in the house. At least she stood a chance with the window.

"Ma'am, are you still there?" the operator asked, but Jennie couldn't focus on her.

Ethan, where are you? I need you now!

"Ma'am?"

"There's a fire. He set the house on fire. I have to go." She disconnected and ran across the room. She slipped into her jacket then shoved her phone into her pocket.

Sick with fear, she headed for the bed and ripped off the sheets, then with trembling hands tried to tie them together.

The room felt like an inferno. Sweat dripped down her forehead. She wanted to yank off her jacket but she'd need it when she went out the window. Smoke rolled under the door, filling the room. Her throat felt as if she'd swallowed razor blades and her chest begged for relief.

A loud crash sounded in the hallway as if the stairs had collapsed. She glanced at the door. Flames curled up under it, seeking fresh wood.

She had no time to finish the sheets. She had to move now or die.

The world in slow motion, she ripped down the blinds and lifted the window. She searched the area, expecting to see a man from the Sotos Cartel with gun drawn and aimed her way. She found only blackness lit with flames from the windows on the first floor.

She crashed a chair through the screen then ducked back inside before a bullet flew through the air.

God, please be with me and keep me safe.

She climbed onto the sill, eyeing the ground below and jumped, hoping, praying, pleading she wasn't leaping to her death.

* * *

Phone to his ear, Ethan grabbed his weapon and keys then headed to the door.

The phone rang for the fourth time.

"C'mon, Cole. Answer." He took a deep breath to keep his frustration over his brother not answering from getting to him.

The call went to voice mail. He hung up then hit Redial and tucked the phone between his ear and shoulder. He slipped his key into the lock and twisted the dead bolt. As if outside his body, he noted his trembling hands and heart beating double, maybe triple, time.

He'd never been so worried in his life. Except maybe when the police came to the door to notify him of his parents' murder. The officers had been waiting for him as he'd pulled into his driveway. Their posture and expressions told him they'd come for a death notification. Ethan just hadn't known who had died.

Third ring.

"What?" Cole grumbled.

"We have an incident. I need you to get back to Kat's house ASAP." Ethan clicked the remote to unlock his truck.

"What happened?" Cole sounded more alert.

"There's someone prowling around the outside of the house."

"Aw, man, you woke me for that? It's probably just

the neighbor's dog again. You know how it likes to dig up Kat's prize roses."

"And if it's the cartel? Do you want to be responsible for what happens to Kat and Jennie if it's more of Sotos's men?" Ethan slid into his truck and revved the engine.

Cole groaned. "I'm on my way, but if it's a false alarm, you owe me."

Ethan chose to ignore the "owing" bit. His gut said this wasn't a false alarm. "If you haul yourself out of bed at a decent speed, you'll easily beat me there."

"I'm already up."

"Good. Call me the minute, and I mean the *minute,* you arrive."

Ethan disconnected and backed out of his parking space at the town-house complex. He raced through the streets, thankful it was so late at night and the usually thick traffic was all but nonexistent. He should gain at least five minutes on the twenty he'd promised Jennie.

He concentrated on driving, weaving around the few cars he did find, pressing the truck to the upper end of safe limits and looking at the clock every few minutes.

Five had passed since he'd hopped into the truck.

God, please keep Kat and Jennie safe. Please. If anyone has to die tonight, let it be me. Don't take another member of my family or the woman I love. Please.

His phone rang from its holder on the dash. Cole.

"What's going on?" Ethan asked, breathless with concern.

"You were right. It's not a false alarm. Someone torched the house and it's completely engulfed in flames."

"What about Jen and Kat?" Ethan asked, not really wanting to know the answer.

"No sign of either of them yet. But hang on, I'm circling the house now. I can't get very close." He sounded out of breath. Ethan knew he was moving fast.

Still, Ethan wanted to push his brother as he was now pushing his gas pedal to the floor, not caring about safe limits anymore.

"Wait," Cole said. "I see someone up ahead."

"And?"

"Can't tell anything from here. I need to put the phone in my pocket now. I have to move some debris to get to whoever it is."

"Get back on the phone as soon as you know anything." Ethan slammed a hand on the wheel.

He was still five minutes out. It was going to be the longest five minutes of his life.

Pain pulled Jennie from darkness. Her skull threatened to explode. Nausea twisted her stomach. She wanted to open her eyes to see where she was but couldn't make the effort. She sensed a steady rhythm of tires rolling over pavement, but that was impossible, wasn't it? She'd just jumped from the bedroom and couldn't be in a car.

Maybe Ethan had arrived, found her injured and arranged for an ambulance. No, she was sitting up, not lying on her back. Was she with Ethan in his truck?

She tried to lift her eyelids again. Heavy. Too heavy. She tried to speak. Her lips wouldn't move.

Lord, You obviously saved me from death in the fall. Thank You. Now please help me.

She listened to the wheels thrumming over the asphalt and waited for the strength to move. She should be jubilant over making it out of the inferno alive and pumped up with adrenaline. Inferno. Poor Kat. Her house was toast.

Wait! Kat. How was Kat? Jennie had to know.

She bore down and forced her mouth to open. "Kat? How's Kat?"

"I don't know, Jen. I didn't see her."

"Wes?" she croaked out through cracked lips. Her throat felt as if she'd swallowed shards of glass, but she forced her head to roll toward the voice then pried her eyes open. "Why..." She couldn't manage any more.

He glanced at her. "I guess you want to know why you're with me."

"Yes," she whispered.

"I left my cell phone at Kat's place. I didn't have her phone number, so I came back to see if anyone was still awake and pick it up." He let out a low whistle. "The house was on fire, and I found you lying on the ground. I scooped you up before the smoke got to you."

"Oh." She thought she said the word, but maybe her mouth just formed it.

"You were unconscious. I wanted to call 9-1-1 and wait for paramedics to arrive, but like I said, I didn't have my phone to call them, so I'm taking you to the E.R." He patted her knee. "You don't know how glad I am that you're moving. I thought maybe you were a goner."

"Kat? Did you find Kat?"

"Ah, no. Sorry. There was no one else around."

Jennie's heart constricted and she wanted to sink back into oblivion. But maybe Kat was all right and Wes just didn't see her.

"Call her," Jennie said.

"I don't have her number."

"My phone. Jacket pocket."

"I really think we should just keep going. I'll call her when we get to the hospital."

"Now!" Jennie shouted, surprised she managed to get the word out so forcefully.

"Okay, relax. I'll pull over and call."

Exhausted, she closed her eyes and felt the car slowing to a stop then Wes retrieving her phone.

"Is she in the directory?" he asked.

"Yes."

"There she is." He hummed and Jennie figured he was waiting for Kat to answer. But how odd to be so calm and humming in a situation that would normally make Wes jumpy.

"Hello, Kat," Wes said then fell silent for a few

moments. "Yeah, she's with me. I'm taking her to the E.R." He paused and then Jennie heard him explain about coming by for his phone. "She's pretty out of it, but we can try." He touched her shoulder. "Jen, she wants to talk to you."

She opened her eyes and he held the phone to her ear. "Kat."

"Oh, my gosh, Jennie. I am so glad to hear your voice."

"Are you okay?"

"Fine. Just a bump on the head." She paused and Jennie could hear her draw in a deep breath. Maybe nausea was wreaking havoc with her, too. "Listen, Jen. I think the cartel must be tracking you though the GPS in your phone. At least, that's the only way I can think of that they could've found you at my house. So I need you to turn it off. And take the battery out just to be sure. Okay?"

"Tell Wes," Jennie said, reaching the last of her reserves.

"Okay," Kat answered. "I'll tell him, and we'll come to the hospital as soon as Ethan gets here."

"Talk to her, Wes." She let her eyes drift closed.

She felt Wes take the phone back and quiet descended on them for a few moments.

"Yeah. OHSU. That's the one." The hospital affiliated with Oregon Health and Science University was one of the best in the city and the closest hospital. "No, we're fine. The car has GPS and it'll take us right there." He disconnected and touched Jennie's knee. "Kat told me to turn off your phone and take out the battery so that's what I'm going to do. Okay?"

"Can you write down her phone number first? Just in case I need to call her from the hospital."

He nodded then found a pen in the console and wrote the number on the back of a receipt.

"Put it in my pocket." She started to relax. Well, as much as her throbbing head would allow. Everything and everyone was okay. She could go to sleep, and when she woke up, she'd see Ethan and his family.

The thought put a smile on her face for a second before the pain was too much.

"Okay. Here we go," Wes said, and Jennie felt the car pull onto the street.

The tires lulled her toward sleep, and thinking of Ethan, she started to drop off. She'd come close to death and she couldn't wait to talk with him. To tell him that he was right. She was hiding behind a wall and she was ready to come out from behind it. To see if they could work as a couple.

Sleep beckoned.

The GPS voice jerked her awake. It said to take the I-405 North ramp.

What? This wouldn't take them to the hospital.

"Where are you going, Wes?"

"Ah, I wondered when you'd figure out we weren't headed to the hospital." He laughed a disturbing laugh. "Too bad you didn't sleep for the whole drive."

By the time she pried open her eyes again, he was

looking at her, his eyes hard and mean. His mouth a slash of anger.

"Remind me to thank Kat for telling me you could be tracked by the GPS in your cell." A flat smile. "Oh, that's right. You won't be alive to remind me, now, will you?"

SEVENTEEN

Ethan jumped from his truck and raced across the street toward Kat. She'd called to tell him Jennie was safe with Wes and his anxiety level had dropped, but physically seeing her was the only thing that would make him completely relax.

Ethan climbed over the barricade and pulled Kat into his arms.

"Don't ever scare me like that again, okay?" he whispered into her smoky hair.

She pulled back with a scowl where the smile had been. "You think this was my fault?"

"Absolutely not. I know you're well trained and did the right thing. I just don't like the fact that my little sister was attacked." He gave her a tight squeeze, and keeping his arm around her shoulder, he moved them toward Cole.

She stepped away and he noticed an angry gash on the back of her head. "This doesn't look good. You need to have this checked out."

"It's nothing."

"It's not nothing," Cole said. "The medics wanted to take you in."

She crossed her arms. "I need to stay here."

"I can take care of things," Cole replied.

Ethan clasped his hand on Kat's arm. "I'll take you."

She shook it off. "And what if I don't want to go?"

"Please." Ethan used a cajoling tone. "I want to go check on Jennie and would like you to ride along with me."

She crossed her arms. "Fine. But I'll decide if I want to have my head looked at."

Not if he had anything to do with it. "I need to borrow your SUV, bro," he said to Cole. "With the way this princess likes to be pampered, my truck won't be too comfortable for her and Jennie both."

Kat socked him and he grabbed her in a good-humored hug as Cole dug out his keys.

Thank You, God, for keeping her safe.

He took the keys and released Kat. "Call us if anything comes up." He shared a concerned look with Cole then took off with Kat.

Once on the road, he glanced at her. She leaned against the door, her posture rigid. She was upset, but she wasn't going to let him see it. Then she'd have to worry about how he was feeling.

Well, he wouldn't let her get away with not talking about this. "I'm sorry about your house, Kat."

She shrugged. "It's no big deal."

"It is a big deal, and you should be upset."

"It's just stuff. It can all be replaced. The important thing is that Jennie's okay."

"Both you and Jen." He shook his head. "I can't tell you how worried I was."

She laid a hand on his arm. "Let's just forget it, okay?"

He nodded, but knew at some point she'd need talk to someone about it. He'd make sure one of them was available to listen.

His phone rang. He glanced at it mounted on the dash. "It's Detective Tilden."

"Calling you instead of me. So much for the brotherhood of police officers."

"Don't get testy, Kat. He must have a reason for calling me instead." He clicked his speaker button. "Detective."

"We got a hit on the prints at the darkroom. Name's Artie Clemmons. Turns out the DEA had his file flagged. He's a cleaner for the Sotos Cartel."

Ethan let out a low whistle.

A cleaner did just what the name suggested. Cleaned up messes. The job usually involved permanently silencing the person who caused the mess. In this case, Jennie.

"I'm guessing you're telling me this because the DEA is looking for help in bringing him in."

"Exactly. They'd like your client to take a look at his mug shot to see if she recognizes him."

"I'm on the way to see her now. Can you email the picture?"

"You got it. Just get back to me tonight so I can get the DEA off my back." His wary tone said he'd had his fill of the Feds breathing down his neck.

"I'll do my best," Ethan promised then punched End. "It'll be interesting to see who this guy is."

Kat peered at him. "*Interesting* isn't the word I'd use."

Ethan caught the worry in his sister's tone and decided it was best not to add to her concern by saying anything more until they could look at the picture. They made the rest of the trip in silence, and at the E.R., Ethan led the way to the duty nurse.

"We're here to see Jennifer Buchanan." He ended with a smile, hoping to ease her harried expression.

"Hold on." She typed on her keyboard then frowned. "We don't have anyone by that name."

"Try Jennie."

His phone chimed. Good. The photo from Tilden. Ethan unlocked the phone.

"Sorry, sir," the nurse said, pulling his attention back. "No Buchanan at all."

"There has to be a mistake."

"No mistake, sir."

He was starting to get miffed. "Maybe she just hasn't been entered in the system yet."

She drew in a deep breath and sighed. "Then she'd still be sitting in the waiting area. No one is allowed in the patient area without being entered in the computer."

Ethan looked at Kat and the concern in her eyes

gave him pause. He was still thinking this was a mistake, but she clearly thought something had happened to Jennie. Kat had done the right thing in telling Jennie to turn off her phone, but right now he wished they could call her and clear this up.

"Where's the waiting room?" he asked.

"Down the hall to your left."

"C'mon," he said to Kat. "Let's make sure she isn't in there."

"And if she isn't?"

"Then I'll make a scene until they agree to let me look for her."

As they walked, he thumbed through the menu on his phone and opened the photo.

He came to a dead stop and held out the phone for Kat.

She gasped. "That's Wes."

"Also known as Artie Clemmons." Ethan stared at the mug shot of Jennie's old boyfriend. "And he has Jennie."

Wes wanted to kill her. Jennie wasn't going to let that happen. She leaned against the door and pretended she'd passed out. She needed to gain her strength if she was going to escape. Escape. How foreign that word was when it came to Wes.

She never saw that coming. When had he hooked up with Sotos? Was it recent? Or was he connected to the gang when they were together?

He'd taken her to Mexico once, not long after his

accident. Left her alone on the main drag and said he had to see a man about a prescription. She'd bought his story. Many Americans saved money by buying prescription drugs in the *farmácias* lining the streets in border towns.

Maybe he wasn't buying prescriptions after all. Maybe he was meeting with Sotos.

She shuddered.

"We're almost there, Jen," Wes said. She hadn't fooled him—he knew she was awake. "The bridge is up ahead."

Almost there. The GPS's directions said he was taking her to Sauvie Island, the same place they'd enjoyed the corn maze. The island was mostly agricultural and recreational with a large wildlife area. At this time of night, the roads were deserted and people who lived on the island were fast asleep.

It made sense that Wes chose to bring her here. There weren't many places in close proximity to Portland where you could kill someone and dump the body without immediate discovery. And there were even fewer places he had visited during his brief stay in Portland when they'd met.

"I really hate to do this," he continued, "but it's all your fault."

Her fault, ha! He had a choice. He didn't have to kill her.

She felt the car slow, and she peeked from under veiled lashes. Good, her eyelids weren't as heavy. Maybe she'd be able to fight when needed.

Wes turned off Highway 30 and crossed the bridge. This was the only route onto the island. Maybe that could help her if Kat and Ethan had gone to the hospital, discovered she was missing and started looking for her.

Had they even arrived at the hospital yet?

Lord, please guide Ethan to me. Keep him safe.

The car turned left and she knew they were heading north, probably heading toward the wildlife preserve. If so, he'd have to slow down to make the curve in the road. That was her chance to bail out of the car. She felt around to see if she was wearing a seat belt. No. Good. It would be easier to get out the door.

She crept her fingers forward on the arm and found the door lock. Holding her finger over it, she took deep breaths to calm her racing heart and oxygenate her blood. The click would give her away. She had to be ready to run when she pushed the button.

She pulled up her knees. Good. Things seemed to be in better working order. Now she simply had to wait for the right moment. Soon the car slowed. She pressed the button, jerked open the door and pushed her body from the moving vehicle.

"What the—?" Wes said and shot out an arm.

She felt his fingers graze her jacket before she tumbled into the ditch and rolled. She tucked into a ball and the gravel bit into her knees, her arms. She came to a stop in a deep puddle.

The car squealed to a stop and then crunched on the gravel shoulder. He was coming after her. Adrenaline flowing, she got to her feet and took off, running blind into the night.

Please, God, help me get away.

Her legs felt as if she'd strapped on weights, but she ran. Over ruts.

Ran. Through scrub.

Ran. Down a hill.

A log grabbed her foot.

She flew through the air.

Pain shot into her ankle. Up her leg. Excruciating.

Wes's footfalls pounded loudly through the field, a flashlight tracking her every move.

Ignore it. Get up. Run.

She jerked to her feet.

Ran. Hard. Through more ruts. Stumbled again and again until her elbows, knees and head were all screaming in pain.

She gasped for breath. Pain stole it away. She couldn't run anymore.

She peered through the darkness. Couldn't see Wes or his light. She looked forward. A copse of trees. About a hundred yards away. She could hide. Had to hide.

Could she get that far without him seeing her? She had to. She turned onto her belly. The earthly scent of the soil rose up to meet her. She dragged herself over the mud.

"You can do it, Jennie. You can make it," she kept whispering to herself.

Mud caked her hands, now raw from clawing through the shrubbery.

Oh, Lord, please.

Hand over hand she pulled. She pushed with her feet.

Made little progress as the mud slowed her down and ripped away her remaining strength.

She kept moving, but only by inches now.

Wes's light found her. The beam dancing over her like a searchlight.

She laid her head on the cold ground, pine needles rough against her cheek.

Lord, please, I need You. Don't let me die.

The prayer hung on her lips, and spent, she waited for her killer to arrive.

EIGHTEEN

"What hotel did Wes say he was staying at?" Ethan demanded. He'd tuned out Wes most of the time, not wanting to face his jealousy. Now it could cost Jennie her life.

Kat laid a hand on his arm and replied with a well-known Portland hotel.

Hope found a glimmer in his heart. "You stay here and get checked out. I'll head to the hotel to see what I can find."

"Not happening, bro. If you're going, I'm going."

"Fine. But don't slow me down." He didn't wait for her but ran for his car. He felt cruel for expecting her to keep up after what she'd just been through, but maybe she'd realize she wasn't fit enough to do this, and she'd head back inside.

But she matched him step for step.

He clicked his locks and they climbed in.

"Maybe we should call this in," Kat offered. "Dispatch could have a uniform at the hotel in minutes."

He glanced at her as he eased out of the space. "A patrol officer wouldn't let us search the room. We're the only ones who can make sense of anything Clemmons left behind."

"We can't just waltz up to the front desk and ask for Clemmons's key. We'll need help gaining access to the room."

He sped up and merged onto the road. "I'd rather not involve someone we don't know in that. Can you call in a favor with Tommy?" Ethan felt certain Kat could convince her old partner to tell the front-desk clerk this was official police business.

"If I can find him, I'm sure he'll meet us there."

"Then call him. But the less he knows about our plans, the better off he'll be." Ethan turned back to his driving and negotiated the deserted streets while listening to Kat talk with Tommy.

"He's on his way." She stowed her phone.

"Good."

Details settled, Ethan couldn't keep his mind off Jennie's fate any longer. His gut was tied in a knot, his heart torn in two. It was bad enough that Clemmons had taken her, but his last personal conversation with her hadn't been positive. Telling her she felt unworthy of love couldn't be the last real conversation he had with her.

Father God. Please don't let things end this way. I love Jennie. How I love her. I need her alive and with me. Please, please, I beg of You, keep her safe until I can find her.

His prayer hung in his mind as he parked in the lot alongside Tommy's Explorer.

This was a positive sign. He'd already gotten there. Ethan and Kat headed for the front door and found Tommy leaning against the wall by the elevator. Over six feet and commanding in a dark suit with white shirt and blue tie, he looked like a businessman staying at the hotel. But his face said he'd seen years of violence on the streets and was wise to it all. From what Kat had told Ethan, Tommy was the epitome of the perfect officer.

Once he knew what they were doing here, would he let them into the room?

Tommy gave Kat a piercing look. "Didn't know you were bringing Ethan."

"Must've forgotten to mention that." She reached out for the key card in Tommy's hand.

He rolled his eyes and held on to it. "Not so fast. Suppose you tell me what this is about before I put my career on the line for you."

"Fill him in on the way up to the room," Ethan said.

Since Tommy was the only one in the group who knew Clemmons's room number, Ethan held out his hand to encourage Tommy to take the lead. They boarded the elevator and Kat gave Tommy the barest of details before they reached the seventh floor and the door slid open.

Outside room 739, Tommy unlocked the door and Ethan bolted past him.

He made a quick visual sweep. Closet empty. Bathroom counter bare. Bed unmade and trash in the can. "He's checked out."

"Looks like it," Kat said and went to the nightstand as Tommy ripped the covers from the bed.

Ethan lifted the trash can and shifted through its contents.

"Receipts." He removed several balled-up bits of paper. "Here's one for gas. Maybe the station has surveillance and we can get a plate number. I'll get Cole working on it."

"I realize you all like to keep things in the family," Tommy said, his tone snarky, "but my team can run this down faster than your brother can."

"Fine." Ethan handed the receipt to Tommy. "If they get a plate and the car's a rental, make sure they contact the company for GPS tracking."

Tommy gave Ethan a well-duh look as all officers knew most rental-car companies attach GPS tracking devices to their cars in the event of theft. "I'll also pull any recent credit-card activity."

"Since this isn't an official case, won't all of this get you in trouble?" Kat asked.

"Maybe." Tommy dialed his phone. "But if what you two say is true, it's better for me to get in trouble than this woman to get killed."

"Tommy," Kat said with a tip of her head at Ethan.

Tommy looked up at Ethan, his expression turning sheepish. "Sorry, man. We'll find her before that happens."

Ethan nodded his agreement, but he knew better. Tommy spoke the truth. Clemmons didn't leave much of a trail, and they'd have to get very lucky if they were going to find Jennie alive.

From the cold, damp earth, Jennie looked up into the beam of Wes's flashlight. The harsh glare left him shadowed and ominous looking, but his gun, aimed at her heart, was fully in focus.

What had happened to the man she'd once shared her life with? Did he still exist in there somewhere? If so she needed to play on their past. Stall for time. If he got her back in that car, she was dead, but if she kept him talking, she might have a chance.

"You're really not going to turn me over to Sotos to kill me are you?" She tried to sound brave, but her voice wavered.

"No."

"So what's this about, then?"

"Just what you think. You wouldn't listen to the warnings and now you have to pay."

"Pay? But I don't understand. If you're not going to turn me over to them, how will I pay?"

He laughed and she felt as if he'd left his body and become some crazed man. "I'm going to do it."

"What? You? You're kidding, right?"

"No."

"This isn't funny, Wes."

"Not meant to be funny. Sotos wants you eliminated and that's what I plan to do." He jerked his head toward the car. "Get up and let's get this over with."

"No. Wait." She took deep breaths to keep her panic

at bay. "You don't want to kill me. I mean, sure, you've probably done some illegal things in the past, but murder? That's a whole other thing."

He laughed again. "Don't be so naive, Jen. This won't be the first time I've cleaned up a problem this way."

She gasped. "You've done this before?" She sucked in air, but it felt too thick to drag in. "How long? Not when we were together."

"Not until we split."

"Why?" she whispered.

"Excitement. Pure and simple. The rush is like no other." His lips curled in a grin. "In fact, I've even planned this for maximum excitement."

"What do you mean?" she asked, hoping he wasn't going to reveal a horrific plan to kill her.

"Back in the car, when you asked to call Kat, I could've faked the call and said it rolled to voice mail. But I didn't. I wanted them to know I have you." He chuckled. "I can see them. Maybe they've figured out who I am and maybe not. But for sure they're frantically running around trying to locate you."

"They will find me and come for me."

His eyes gleamed. "I hope they do, too. Nothing better than a chase. It's all a part of the fun, Jen. All part of the fun."

"Let me go, Wes. You can find a thrill elsewhere."

He shook his head. "It doesn't work that way, Jen. You angered one of the most dangerous men alive. I'm not risking his wrath for you." He moved toward her. "Now, get up, or I'll drag you up."

She shifted to her knees and searched the area for an escape route.

He clamped a hand on her elbow and jerked her into a standing position. Pain radiated through her knee and her head throbbed. He shoved her forward and she stumbled but righted herself.

"Just tell me one more thing," she said, desperately trying to stall him as they neared his car. "How did Sotos even know about the picture?"

His feet stilled and a cruel smile swept over his mouth. "I told him."

"You?" Jennie said. "How did you know?"

"The local paper ran a story about your show and included a few of your pictures. I recognized Sotos's car in the background of one of them."

"You could tell it was his car?" she asked, wondering how they'd missed seeing this in their search of the photos.

"He's got a one-of-a-kind hood ornament. A gold medallion with a snake on it. Figured if his car was there so was he and maybe you caught him in a picture, too. So I warned him."

Jennie looked up at him. "I can't believe you'd betray me like that."

He laughed. "That's why I left you, sweetheart. You have no imagination."

She just stared at him. "Everything is starting to make sense. When Ethan kept me hidden from the cartel, they sent you here to find me and keep tabs on me. That's how they found me at Bitsy's and then Kat's house, isn't it?"

"So glad you recognize my fine work." He took a bow.

Disgusted, she turned away and took a few steps toward the car.

"Don't think I'm a fool, Jen." He jerked her to a stop. "You won't be riding up front again."

He popped the trunk with the remote and dragged her to the rear of the car. She tried not to lose hope. To remember what Ethan had promised. He'd said he'd be there for her for as long as she needed him. She really needed him now. Needed his arms wrapped around her, him telling her everything would be okay.

Wes gave her a shove until her leg connected with the cold bumper then he held the gun to her temple. "Get in."

The metal bit into her skin like a branding iron. She wanted to fight him, but her only hope was to go along and try to escape again. She climbed into the dark, cavernous space and looked up at him.

He cast a snide smile in her direction and lifted his hand to close the trunk.

She'd seen her share of TV shows with people found dead in the trunk.

Her heart refused to beat, but she returned his look with a brave one. As the trunk closed, she felt certain she'd need more than bravery to save her life.

NINETEEN

Ethan paced the floor of Clemmons's hotel room. Tommy had his phone pressed to his ear, and Kat kept giving Ethan sidelong glances in her mothering way.

He'd like to reassure her that he'd be fine but honestly, if they didn't find Jennie, he may not survive. And standing around here wasn't doing him any good.

"We might as well leave," he said to Kat. "There's nothing here."

"And go where?" she asked.

"I don't know, but I can't just sit here and twiddle my thumbs." He shook his head. "I can't lose her again, Kat."

"Hey, c'mon." She rested a hand on his shoulder. "We'll find her."

The sweet gesture didn't help stem the fear rising out of control. "How?"

"I don't know, but God has heard our prayers and He'll lead us."

"Trouble is, He doesn't always have the same plans

as we do." He clutched Kat's hand. "Case in point, our parents."

"Don't think that way, Ethan. It won't help. You've got to stay strong."

Ethan knew that, but he also knew what a cold-blooded killer like Clemmons was capable of doing.

"We've got a plate," Tommy announced. "Car's a rental. We're running down the GPS now."

Ethan felt a surge of relief. Good, they'd find her. But she'd been gone over an hour. Clemmons could've taken her out of the city. Only way to find her in time would be with a helicopter.

"We might need a chopper." Ethan grabbed his phone and dialed Derrick, whose friend owned a helicopter. If the buddy wasn't available, Derrick was a certified pilot. Thank goodness Dani had taken over the detail with Madeline, or he'd be in town and not at his home near the airport.

"No time for questions," he said the minute Derrick answered. "I'm downtown and we need a chopper now. Can you make it happen?"

"You know I can." Excitement colored his tone. "There's a public heliport at First and Davis. It's on top of the parking structure. I'll meet you there. You'll need a code for the elevator to access the helipad." Derrick rattled it off.

Ethan grabbed a pen and wrote the numbers on his hand. "Thanks, little bro. See you there."

"Let's roll, people." Ethan stepped toward the door.

Kat and Tommy followed him into the hallway and to the elevator. They boarded and the tiny space made Ethan feel as if he was going to jump out of his skin.

C'mon, c'mon, c'mon. Hurry up already.

The doors parted and he bolted out like a gunshot. Outside, he breathed deep of the cool night air, which did little to ease his panic.

"If we take my car, we can run the lights," Tommy said, taking the lead and jogging to his car. He clicked the locks and jumped in.

Ethan jerked open the back door for Kat and climbed in after her. No one spoke as the miles flew by.

The tension was palpable in the air. At one point, Ethan thought it might smother him.

Kat's phone jangled, and he jumped.

She pulled it from her jacket pocket and glanced at it.

"No one I know. But I should answer in case it's related to the case. Hello," Kat said into the phone, then listened. Her mouth dropped open, and she put her hand over the phone. "It's Jennie."

"Jennie? How?" Ethan ripped the phone from his sister's hand. "Jen."

"Ethan." A soft whisper echoed in his head like a clanging bell.

"Jen. Is that really you?"

"Yes." One word, but filled with despair.

"Thank God. With your cell off, I didn't think we'd ever hear from you."

"I found one of those GoPhones in Wes's tote bag." Her relief flowed through the phone.

"Are you all right, Jen? Where are you?"

"In the trunk of Wes's car. He's a killer, Ethan."

"I know, honey, but we'll get to you before he can hurt you." He forced confidence into his tone that he didn't feel. "Where's he taking you?"

"Someplace on Sauvie Island."

He put his hand over the phone. "Get us to that chopper, Tommy. They're on Sauvie Island." He lifted his hand. "Did he hurt you, Jen?"

"Not yet. But he says he's going to kill me."

"I won't let him."

"I don't see how you'll stop him. It'll take you too long to get here." She started to whimper.

"Don't cry, Jen. We have a chopper on standby. We're heading for it right now," he said, but his heart tightened.

"But then what? It's dark. How can you possibly tell which car I'm in?"

She had a point. He frowned, trying to think. There wouldn't be much traffic, but still, they needed a signal. Something to distinguish Clemmons's car from any others on the road. A signal Jennie could provide from inside the trunk.

"Ethan?" she pleaded.

"I'm thinking, honey," he answered and peered at the car ahead hitting the brakes.

"That's it," he shouted. "Listen carefully, Jen. I need you to kick out one of the taillights. Can you do that?"

"I'll try." She fell silent, and he heard her moving around.

Tommy pulled into the parking garage. Ethan didn't wait for the car to come to a complete stop but when Tommy slowed, Ethan leaped out. The whir of chopper blades split the night. Good, they had a chance.

He ran for the elevator. Tommy's and Kat's footfalls pounded behind him. He punched in the code and the elevator jolted up.

"Got it, Ethan. I got it. It worked." Jennie panted for breath but her voice held a tinge of hope.

"Good. We're on our way, Jen. We're in the elevator to the helipad."

The door slid open. Tommy and Kat burst onto the helipad and Ethan hung back.

"I'm boarding the chopper now," he said to Jennie. "With the noise, we won't be able to talk, but do you still want to stay connected?"

"Yes, please."

Her desperation climbed up his back and sat on him like the weight of the world. He tried to breathe, but he felt as if he were suffocating with fear.

"I love you, Jen," he said then bolted outside. The whirring rotors tore away her answer, but he didn't care. The only thing that mattered right now was that he find her and keep her alive. Everything else could be worked out.

* * *

Ethan nestled the phone on his lap and sat on the edge of the front seat. Derrick piloted the old aircraft. A bulky headset allowed Ethan to communicate with Derrick sitting beside him, and Tommy and Kat, who occupied the backseats.

Ethan peered through binoculars into the black night. Fat lot of good they did him. Endless miles of darkness loomed ahead, the ground encased in a thick fog, but he kept searching. He wished their chopper was equipped with searchlights, but few helicopters outside of law enforcement had such equipment.

Ethan swiveled and squinted. "Over there. To my right. That car has only one taillight," he said, hoping it wasn't his imagination.

"Affirmative," Tommy answered.

"I see it, too," Kat said.

"Get in position to land on the road," Ethan barked at Derrick. "Set down in front of them."

"Hold on," Tommy said. "You don't have clearance to land on a public road."

"Do as I said, Derrick." Ethan hoped his big-brother tone would usurp Tommy. "I'm not waiting for clearance."

"At least wait until I can get some uniforms to block off the road," Tommy pleaded.

"No time." Ethan lifted the headset from one ear and cupped his hand around the phone. "I see you, Jen. We'll be there in less than a minute."

No reply.

"Jen. Can you hear me?"

Silence.

"Jen," he screamed, drawing Kat's attention.

"Jen's not answering," he shouted.

"Maybe she doesn't have a signal out here or maybe she can't hear you over the noise," Kat answered.

Too bad he couldn't embrace her optimism right now. Too many things could've happened to Jennie since the time he last talked to her. "We need to get this thing on the ground now!"

The chopper banked left and descended. Ethan wished for a spotlight so he could see the car more clearly, but they'd just have to go in with what they had.

"Let me handle this when we land," Tommy said.

Ethan shook his head. "Not a chance."

He turned around and laid a hand on Kat's knee, hoping to communicate his need to be the first one out of the chopper. He hoped Kat would make that happen by slowing Tommy's exit.

She squeezed his hand, but he had no idea what she meant by it.

"I'm gonna fly over and come back at him," Derrick said. "That way you'll be facing him."

Derrick made good on his promise, expertly landing on the road far enough ahead to give Clemmons room to make a sudden stop.

Ethan was out of the chopper and on the road while Clemmons's car was still moving. Gun in hand, he rushed forward as the car screeched to a stop.

Clemmons hopped out and ran to the back of the

car. He opened the trunk, and by the time Ethan could see Jennie's terrified face lit by the trunk light, Clemmons had his weapon planted on her temple.

"Back off or she's toast."

Ethan lifted up his hands. "Don't do anything rash, Clemmons."

"Clemmons?" Jennie asked as she climbed out.

"Oh, yeah. I forgot to mention. When I changed my line of work, I changed my name, too. Wouldn't want my parents to be upset if I ever got busted." He laughed.

The urge to attack this creep bit into Ethan's mind, but common sense held him in place. He heard footfalls heading down the road.

"Tell your buddies to get back in the chopper," Clemmons screamed, sounding as if he were losing it. He jerked Jennie closer and shoved the gun into her temple.

"Do as he says," Ethan commanded, his eyes never leaving Jennie's terror-filled face.

Their footfalls retreated.

"Now we'll be going." Clemmons started backing away, using Jennie as a shield.

"Think this through, Clemmons. Half the Portland police force is on the way. You can make a deal. Roll over on Sotos."

Clemmons snorted. "Nice try, but you know as well as I do Sotos has a long arm. I'd be dead before the ink dried on the agreement."

"The police can protect you."

"Right. I've been cleaning up Sotos's messes for far too long to believe that." At least he admitted to working with Sotos.

Clemmons started moving again. "Don't follow us or I'll put a bullet through her pretty little head."

"Jen." Her name whispered out, and Ethan saw the joy on Clemmons's face.

"It's okay, Ethan," Jennie said, her voice hoarse. "Always remember our days at the beach. Remember the sidewinder." She forced a laugh.

The sidewinder, the move he and his siblings inflicted on each other at the beach? The move he'd taught Jennie to prepare her for the trick one of his siblings was likely to play. A quick sweep of the leg and the target went crashing into the water.

"You do remember it, don't you?" she asked now, just steps away from the ditch.

She wasn't going to use it on Clemmons, was she? "Yes, of course, but—"

"It always works, Ethan. Always." The determination in her tone told him that she was.

"No, Jen."

"Shut up," Clemmons snarled.

"Now," Jennie yelled and swept out her foot.

Clemmons lost his footing. He tumbled backward, his gun aimed at Jennie. A shot rang out.

"No!" Ethan shouted and curled his finger, firing at Clemmons.

Another shot ricocheted through the air, and Jennie crumbled to the ground.

TWENTY

Ethan ran across the road. He wanted to scoop Jennie into his arms, but he needed to make sure Clemmons couldn't hurt them. He pressed his finger against Clemmons's throat. No pulse.

Ethan had killed someone. Guilt started to rise, but he forced it down. He'd regret that this happened, but he'd not feel guilt. Clemmons hadn't given him a choice.

He scrambled over to Jennie, gently lifted her into his arms and looked for any sign of life. Her chest rose and fell.

Good. She was breathing.

"Is she okay?" Kat came running up with her flashlight lighting her path, Tommy hot on her heels.

"I don't know." His arm felt sticky and wet. "Shine your light over here."

Tommy went to check Clemmons, and Kat squatted next to him.

The flashlight's beam passed over his blood-covered arm and landed on Jennie's head, oozing more.

"Did he shoot her?" Kat ripped off her jacket and pressed it against Jennie's head.

Ethan didn't want to waste precious time locating the site of her injury. Or if he were honest, he didn't want to know if she had a bullet in her head.

"We need to get her to the hospital," Kat said.

"I'm getting up. Keep your hand on her head." He slowly rose.

His legs wobbly from fear, they hurried to the helicopter. He climbed in back with Jennie and sat on the floor so he didn't need to let go of her. With his free hand, he held Kat's jacket in place, but felt the blood continuing to saturate the fabric.

"OHSU, Derrick, and make it fast," Kat said, taking a front seat.

Derrick took off and Ethan cradled Jennie in his arms. He watched her face, dimly lit by the many lights on the instrument panel. He heard Derrick in the background, notifying the hospital of Jennie's injury and their ETA.

The unthinkable came to Ethan's mind and he felt as if his heart was ripping in two.

Had he finally come to admit he didn't want to live without her just to find out he'd have to?

Jennie woke to the sound of heated male voices. She opened her eyes, the bright light closing them again. She forced them open and glanced around.

The hospital. She was in the hospital. Ethan, his

back to her, stood at the far end of the room, his hands fisted, and a tall, lanky man she didn't know faced her. His narrowed eyes were fixed on Ethan, his face ruddy as if angry.

"That's not good enough," Ethan said in a sharp tone. "If the DEA doesn't arrest Eduardo Sotos, he'll send another goon after Jennie."

"And like I told you about a hundred times, we have no physical evidence on Sotos. We can't just arrest him because a man we think is affiliated with his organization tried to kill her."

"Oh, come on, Unger." Ethan spit out the man's name as if it were poison. "Clemmons admitted it in front of several witnesses. What more do you need?"

"I don't know, maybe evidence?" His tone held a liberal dose of sarcasm. "As a former Fed you know that. Our only hope was Clemmons's testimony, but since he died..."

As his words fell off, Jennie tried not to panic, but this was what she'd worried about. Wes—or whatever he called himself—was dead, but there'd be another creep taking his place. And she'd still be running for her life.

"Fine. I know that." Ethan shoved his fingers into his hair. "But it doesn't mean I like it."

"Hey, I hear you. But it is what it is."

"So how about doing your job and getting something on Sotos so he can be arrested?"

"Like we haven't been trying to do that for years."

Again with the sarcasm. "Look, man. I understand your concern. The best thing I can suggest is witness protection."

Jennie gasped. She couldn't go into witness protection. Not now. Not when she'd finally decided to let go of her past and pursue Ethan.

Ethan's eyes met hers and they softened. He turned back to the agent. "We'll talk about this later." His tone was dismissive and Unger left the room.

Ethan stepped to Jennie. "You're awake."

She nodded, but her head throbbed and a wave of dizziness crashed into her. She reached up. Found a bandage circling her head.

"You hit your head when you collapsed."

"How long have I been out?"

"You've been in and out for the last twelve hours or so."

"Twelve hours," she repeated as she tried to think of what she might have missed for half a day. She bolted upright. "The show. I've got to get to work if I'm gonna make the show."

"Relax." He gently settled her back against the pillow. "I found the online backup file with your pictures, and team Justice has been working on reprints for hours."

"But I need to—"

"All you need to do is rest so you have enough strength to attend the opening tomorrow night." He smiled down on her. "The prints won't equal the quality of yours, but you saved all your edits in the files, and that will have to be good enough for once."

She cast him a skeptical glance.

"I know you like things to be perfect, but the show can go on without you, you know. And you're not the only one who can help these children. Others can get involved and take some of the burden from you."

He was right. She could step back and let others get involved. She didn't need to do it all anymore, but could she follow through and let others take the reins so she could spend time finding her own happiness? That might take some getting used to.

"I'll have to think about how to cut back."

"You don't sound convinced of that."

"I am. It's just…" She didn't want to tell him that she didn't know how to live a life free from all the baggage she'd been carrying for years. To be happy. To be content.

"Jen?" He locked gazes with her. "What is it? What's wrong?"

"Nothing."

"I'm pretty sure I know what this is all about, and I think I can help." He sat on the edge of the bed and took a deep breath. "Remember at the bank when I told you about my friend, the one who urged me to forgive you for leaving?"

"Yeah, but I—"

"That was my birth mother," he jumped in. "She felt just like you do until she realized God would never condemn her for her mistake of getting pregnant out of wedlock. She was the one doing that. He didn't come to this world to condemn, Jen." He enveloped her hands in warmth. "You made a mistake. Had a baby. Did the right thing for her. You shouldn't feel guilty. If God can forgive you, why can't you forgive yourself?"

"Um, actually, I was going to say that thanks to you and your family, I've already reached that conclusion."

"So if you've let that go, then why the serious face?"

"I was just wondering if after all these years of focusing on Photos of Hope, I could cut back and find some time for a life of my own."

"And what conclusion did you come to?"

"It's going to be hard, but last night, before the fire, I realized that being alone isn't good. I want a big, boisterous family like yours surrounding me. And I want to start by finding Natalie." She felt all of the old anxiety return.

"What's wrong?" he asked.

"What if Natalie hates me just like you did your birth mother for so long?"

"Then she's foolish like I once was, and we need to work with her to accept the truth." He smiled. "I've had the best life ever, Jen. I didn't suffer from being adopted. Maybe I once thought I did, but I didn't. Your daughter hasn't suffered, either. Let go of the worry."

He studied her with eyes that were warm yet invasive, as if he could see her every thought. And she was beginning to think he could. More than any other man she'd ever known, there was a natural connection between them. As if God made them for each other and wanted them to be together.

"Jen, I…" He looked down toward their hands still twined together.

What did he want to tell her that he was so afraid to say?

Her heart beat double time. "What? What is it?"

"Cole stopped by before you woke up to tell me he found her. Natalie. I asked him to look for her, and he found her this morning. She still lives in Springbrook with Grace and Bill Young."

Jennie jerked her hand free. "You had no right."

"When you love someone, you want to do what you think is best for them."

"You can't possibly know what's best for me."

"Maybe I'll make some mistakes along the way. We all do. But I promise to use love as my motivation all the time."

He'd said he loved her. Twice. No, three times, if she counted the time before he boarded the helicopter. He'd risked his life for her. Hadn't she learned anything? She couldn't keep attacking everyone who tried to help her. Especially not him.

He reached for her hand again, and that impossibly tight knot in her chest loosened.

"I realize you've pretty much been alone all your life. You've had no one to depend on and had to take care of yourself. But you're not alone anymore. I'm here with you." With his free hand, he traced a finger down the side of her face. "For life if you'll let me."

Could she believe him? Did he really want to be with her?

"Don't run away from me again, Jen. Don't hide behind that wall. We're meant to be together. When I saw you crumble to the ground, I felt—" He drew in a deep breath. "It was like someone ripped out my heart and nothing else mattered anymore. Nothing but you. I love you so much."

"And you're sure this is love?"

"Why do you doubt it?"

"I know you feel sorry for me. For the way I was raised. You're a good man, Ethan. Kind, compassionate, caring. Maybe you're mistaking sympathy for love."

He cupped her cheek. "Sure I feel bad about your past, but your past doesn't make my heart beat faster, and it sure doesn't make me want to kiss you. To never let you out of my sight. To be with you forever. That's love. Plain and simple." He smiled, a devastating little grin that sent her heart tumbling. "All I need to be happy is for you to say you love me, too." His face creased in a lost-little-boy look, timid and unsure.

"I do, Ethan."

"Does this mean you'll marry me?"

She stilled. "I'm not used to letting anyone in or having someone worry about me."

He slid closer and laid warm hands on her shoulders. "As long as you promise not to run when you get spooked, we'll be fine. I couldn't survive if I thought you'd ever leave me again."

"I won't, Ethan. Never. I promise." Her words came out as breathless as she felt.

His arms went around her, pulling her close. She grimaced at the pain, but didn't let on. With the warmth flowing through her heart, erasing years of loneliness, physical pain would not stop her from enjoying her dream coming true.

He eased back and his eyes seemed to devour her face. "I love you so much, Jen, and I'll never let you get away from me again. Never."

Her heart swelled with love that should erase everything else, but his talk of *never* brought the future to mind.

"What's wrong?" he asked, squeezing her hand.

"That man who was just here."

"Unger? He's a DEA agent."

"He said something about witness protection. If that happens, I could never ask you to come with me."

"It's not going to happen, honey." His tone wasn't very convincing.

"But if it does?"

He cupped her face, running his thumbs over her cheekbones. "Don't think about that now. Not now. Just think about this."

His voice trailed off and he settled his lips over hers.

She leaned into his kiss and tried to forget all the uncertainty, but as much as she wanted to, she couldn't let go of the thought that she'd just found this man and she would have to run from him again.

Run into protective custody, where she'd never ask this wonderful man to go.

In the gallery bathroom, Kat finished applying makeup to Jennie's neck. When they'd arrived for the show, the lighting highlighted a nasty bruise Jennie had gotten when she was thrown into the trunk. Kat, the ever prepared, grabbed Jennie's hand and dragged her off to the bathroom to remedy the problem.

"There," Kat said and stood back. "No one will be able to see that you've been beaten up."

"Thanks, Kat." Jennie looked in the mirror and smiled at Kat's reflection. "For this and for all the hours you and the other Justices spent working on the photos."

"We did a good job, if I do say so myself."

"Actually, you did. So good, I know that I don't have to take care of every detail of the shows anymore. Maybe I won't need to do as much traveling and will be home more often."

"I'm so excited to have another sister." Kat grabbed Jennie's hands and squeezed.

Jennie's heart bubbled up with happiness, but she wouldn't fully let it take hold. Not until Natalie was back in her life and Eduardo Sotos was no longer a threat. For the past day, Ethan had refused to discuss the continued threat, acting as if Sotos wouldn't still come after her, but she knew it was just a matter of time before he attacked again.

How amazing it would be not to have this threat

hanging over her and to finally have the life of her dreams. To gain not only the man she loved, but a big, boisterous family. A family who, when Ethan announced they were getting married, embraced her like a long-lost sister. It was better than even she could have dreamed. How could she have ever imagined she couldn't fit in with this group?

"So, let's go meet your public."

Public. Who cared about the public tonight?

Not with Sotos still free. And most importantly, with Natalie arriving any minute now. Ethan had invited her and she had agreed to attend. Jennie was going to meet her daughter. Now. Tonight.

She quickly glanced in the mirror then passed her hand over her hair and, with nerves tingling, followed Kat.

Ethan faced the bathroom door, his eyes watchful and concerned. When she smiled, he floored her with a dazzling smile of his own. Her heart fluttered and she felt almost giddy. This man. This wonderful man loved her. Just like she was. Flawed. A sinner. And she'd never felt so whole in her life.

She crossed over to him and he slid an arm around her waist, pulling her close.

"Have I told you how beautiful you look tonight?" he whispered, his breath tickling her neck. "Because if I haven't, I better tell you before all the other guys here start hitting on you and I'm forgotten."

She peered up at him, everyone around them fading into the background. "You *have* told me, and you know it."

He winked and cupped the side of her face. "Yeah, but you can never be too careful when the woman you love is the most beautiful woman in the room."

She felt the heat of his gaze warm her face. She didn't care if the room was filled with other people, but rose on her toes and kissed him. He tightened his hold, drawing her so close she could hardly breathe. This felt so right. So good. Just like she'd dreamed of when life had dealt her yet another blow.

With a groan, he set her away.

"This is not a good idea." His breathing was ragged. "We need to focus on something else or I'll never get through the night."

Her effect on his emotions was heady and she smiled.

"And don't smile at me like that, either." He offered a mock chastisement.

"So," she said innocently, "what do you want to talk about?"

"I got a call from Unger while you were in there primping."

Her good mood whooshed away like a deflating balloon.

"Sorry," he said. "I didn't mean to put that look on your face."

"What did he say?"

"Sotos is in prison."

"What?" her voice shot up and people swiveled to stare at her, but she didn't care. "How?"

"Unger couldn't share many details, and in fact, he claimed it was all hypothetical."

"Tell me everything you know." She felt breathless with urgency.

"Unger started our conversation by saying Sotos has been arrested and is in a secure Mexican prison. And that he won't ever be released. So I asked him how it happened, and he said he wasn't at liberty to share the details."

"But he did tell you something, right?"

"This is the hypothetical part. He said suppose someone high up in the DEA paid a visit to a high-ranking official in Mexico's federal police. An official like the one you caught in your picture. And suppose this official was told to turn on Sotos and arrest him or they'd expose his connection to Sotos and the official could be sure he'd never leave a Mexican prison again."

"So the DEA went to Maceno and convinced him to turn on Sotos."

"Hypothetically." He grinned.

"This is all over, then. I don't have to go into witness protection. I'm free to be with you and Natalie, and Sotos will never come after me again?"

"Never again, Jen." He ended with a cute crooked smile that sent her heart racing.

Thank You, Father. Thank You.

She jumped up and threw her arms around his neck. He held her close and spun her around. "Now nothing can stand in the way of our happiness."

Natalie. Her daughter came to mind. She'd be here any minute and she could still reject her.

Jennie slipped out of Ethan's arms. She tried to keep her worry from her face as she looked toward the door.

She caught sight of a girl whose face resembled the one Jennie stared at every day in the mirror and threatened to stop her heart. She wore a fashionable dress and heels, her blond hair cut stylishly.

Jennie pushed away from Ethan. "She's here."

He turned.

Jennie bit her lip. "What if she doesn't like me? Or what if she's coming here to tell me off?"

"There's nothing not to like about you." He took her hand. "And her parents told me she wants to meet you as much as you want to meet her."

"But this is so public."

"Only for the initial introduction. Then you can move to Madeline's conference room and see all the photo albums I asked Natalie's mother to bring." He gave her a quick hug.

It didn't help. She was so afraid Natalie wouldn't like her, or worse would hate her.

"Think of it like dating," he continued. "Didn't you ever go out to lunch instead of dinner because it was less threatening and easier to get out of?"

She nodded, but nervousness still had her nails biting into her palms and she stared at his chest.

He tipped her face up. "This is the same thing. If it's overwhelming for either of you, you can excuse yourself."

Natalie came closer with graceful steps that Jennie could never manage in heels so high.

"Natalie." The name whispered out of Jennie's mouth, taking the last of her breath away.

Her daughter stood before her. At long last. The tiny infant she'd held only for the briefest of time had grown into a beautiful young woman. More beautiful than Jennie could've imagined. And Jennie had missed the transformation. Tears mounted.

"Hi," Natalie said sweetly then looked at the floor.

She's looking away. Maybe Ethan was wrong and she really doesn't want to meet me after all.

"And you must be Natalie's parents." Ethan held out his hand to the striking couple standing behind Natalie and introduced himself. "Thank you for being so open to this meeting."

Natalie's father smiled warmly and offered his hand to Jennie. "I'm not sure if you remember me. Bill Young. It's good to see you again."

Mrs. Young stood back, seeming more ill at ease. Jennie could fully understand her trepidation, so she smiled at her old English teacher and waited for her to make the next move, but she simply looked away.

"You remember my wife, Grace." Bill put a hand on her back and seemed to force her forward.

She quickly shook Jennie's hand and gave her a tight smile then eased back.

Natalie looked up at Jennie, flashed a tentative smile and looked away again.

Jennie had to say something. Had to break the ice.

"I'm happy to meet you, Natalie. I've thought about this day for so long. I can't believe it's happening, and I finally get to see what a beautiful young lady you've become."

Natalie's face colored, but she smiled in earnest now. "I'm happy to meet you, too."

An uneasy quiet descended and time ticked slowly by.

"Have you all had a chance to look at Jennie's photos yet?" Ethan jumped in.

"We just arrived," Bill answered.

"Maybe you want to have a quick look around and then we'll meet in, say, fifteen minutes in the conference room."

Bill nodded. "Sounds like a plan."

"No, wait," Natalie said, her eyes wide. "You do want to meet with me, right? I mean, you asked, and I'm here and I want to talk." Her words tumbled out on top of each other.

Jennie moved closer and took Natalie's hand. "I think Ethan was trying to let us catch our breath. But I don't need a break. I've been waiting for this day since I had to give you up, and I want to know all about you."

"Me, too." She laughed, a sweet, high melody. "I mean since I was old enough to wonder about you."

Jennie heard Grace draw in a sharp breath.

Natalie went to her mother. "It's okay, Mom." She took Grace's hand. "You'll always be my mom, and I can't do this without you."

Grace smiled, but it didn't blossom into a full-fledged grin.

"You can follow me to the conference room." Jennie turned and led the way.

Ethan caught up to her. "You have a very lovely daughter, Jen. I can't wait to get to know her and make her part of our family."

She shot a quick look at him.

"What? You are planning to have a family with me, aren't you?"

"Of course, I just haven't thought that far into the future yet."

"You better start thinking about it. If we're going to have a house full of kids, we don't have a lot of time to wait." He gave her a mischievous grin. "I mean, at your advanced age we have no time to lose."

She gave him a playful punch to his shoulder, and he grabbed her hand then twined his fingers through hers.

She heard the tight clicks of Natalie's heels on the rough brick floor behind them and the sound overflowed her heart already full with happiness that Ethan brought to her life. At the door, she and Ethan paused, letting Natalie and her family go into the room before them.

She was standing here, the only man she'd ever loved warmly clasping her hand, and after so many years of crying over and wondering about her daughter, she was now here, too. Jennie would never let either one of them disappear from her life again. Never.

* * * * *

Dear Reader,

Thank you for reading Ethan and Jennie's story. I really enjoyed bringing you their struggles and especially liked adding the thread in the book that talks about how we Christians can use our struggles and problems to help others.

I suffer from a chronic illness and because of that, I have challenges in my life on a daily basis. Challenges that some days I'd rather not have. But if I stop and look at it, I see how much the illness requires me to let go of myself and depend on God. And it has given me such compassion for sick and hurting people, which allows me to understand and help them in ways I couldn't do without the suffering. I hope this story has helped you see the same opportunities in your own life.

I love to hear from readers and you can reach me through my website, www.susansleeman.com, or in care of Love Inspired Books at 233 Broadway, Suite 1001, New York, NY 10279.

Susan Sleeman

Questions for Discussion

1. Jennie lives with condemnation for a mistake she made years ago. Have you ever lived with such condemnation? If so, how did you handle it?

2. Jennie and Ethan have both been rejected many times and fear trusting another person with their heart. Have you ever experienced such fear? What can you take away from this story to help you in that relationship?

3. Why do you think it took Jennie so long to believe that she is worthy of love?

4. Which character in the story do you relate most to and why?

5. Jennie had a difficult childhood, but it has given her a heart for helping children. Is there something in your past or even something you are going through right now that you can use to help others in a similar situation?

6. Jennie is terrified of letting anyone see the poverty she grew up in. Do you have anything in your past that you are embarrassed about and are hiding from others?

7. Ethan forgave Jennie for leaving him because he knew that he couldn't harbor resentment toward her. Is there someone you are withholding forgiveness from? If so, can you embrace God's forgiveness and let the pain go?

8. For many years, Ethan didn't believe his mother gave him up for adoption because she loved him. Has there been a time in your life when someone did something out of love, but you are still struggling to believe love motivated it? If so, has Ethan's story helped you see it differently?

9. After reading *Double Exposure,* are you able to look at the misery in your life differently and see it as a way to help others?

10. When Jennie was young, she ran from Ethan because she was afraid to tell him about the baby she gave up. Have you ever run from something that you should've faced head-on? How would it have ended differently if you'd stayed and hadn't run?

11. Families are wonderful and Jennie is thrilled to become a part of the Justice family, but we all know families can also be complicated. If you have siblings as Ethan does, can you see some similarities in your relationships? Have any of your siblings tried to protect you as fiercely as Kat tried to protect Ethan?

12. After the loss of their adoptive parents, Ethan and his siblings decided to work together to help others. This was a major change in their lives. Have you ever suffered a loss that profoundly changed your approach to life? If so, what changes did you make?

LARGER-PRINT BOOKS!

GET 2 FREE
LARGER-PRINT NOVELS
PLUS 2 FREE
MYSTERY GIFTS

Love Inspired®

SUSPENSE
RIVETING INSPIRATIONAL ROMANCE

Larger-print novels are now available...

LARGER-PRINT BOOKS!

**GET 2 FREE
LARGER-PRINT NOVELS
PLUS 2 FREE
MYSTERY GIFTS**

Love Inspired®

Larger-print novels are now available...

YES! Please send me 2 FREE LARGER-PRINT Love Inspired® novels and my 2 FREE mystery gifts (gifts are worth about $10). After receiving them, if I don't wish to receive any more books, I can return the shipping statement marked "cancel". If I don't cancel, I will receive 6 brand-new novels every month and be billed just $4.99 per book in the U.S. or $5.49 per book in Canada. That's a saving of at least 23% off the cover price. It's quite a bargain! Shipping and handling is just 50¢ per book in the U.S. and 75¢ per book in Canada.* I understand that accepting the 2 free books and gifts places me under no obligation to buy anything. I can always return a shipment and cancel at any time. Even if I never buy another book, the two free books and gifts are mine to keep forever.

122/322 IDN FEG3

Name	(PLEASE PRINT)	
Address		Apt. #
City	State/Prov.	Zip/Postal Code

Signature (if under 18, a parent or guardian must sign)

Mail to the **Reader Service:**
IN U.S.A.: P.O. Box 1867, Buffalo, NY 14240-1867
IN CANADA: P.O. Box 609, Fort Erie, Ontario L2A 5X3

Not valid to current subscribers to Love Inspired Larger-Print books.

**Are you a current subscriber to Love Inspired books
and want to receive the larger-print edition?
Call 1-800-873-8635 or visit www.ReaderService.com.**

* Terms and prices subject to change without notice. Prices do not include applicable taxes. Sales tax applicable in N.Y. Canadian residents will be charged applicable taxes. Offer not valid in Quebec. This offer is limited to one order per household. All orders subject to credit approval. Credit or debit balances in a customer's account(s) may be offset by any other outstanding balance owed by or to the customer. Please allow 4 to 6 weeks for delivery. Offer available while quantities last.

Your Privacy—The Reader Service is committed to protecting your privacy. Our Privacy Policy is available online at www.ReaderService.com or upon request from the Reader Service.

We make a portion of our mailing list available to reputable third parties that offer products we believe may interest you. If you prefer that we not exchange your name with third parties, or if you wish to clarify or modify your communication preferences, please visit us at www.ReaderService.com/consumerschoice or write to us at Reader Service Preference Service, P.O. Box 9062, Buffalo, NY 14269. Include your complete name and address.

LILP11B